DIVAS DEATH AND DRAG

Drag Queen Detective 2

SHANE K MORTON

Contents

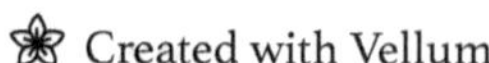 Created with Vellum

I want to thank Deb Swietek for being the best Beta Reader in the World as always. Your guidance is always appreciated. Leona Windwalker, thank you for all your guidance and help. I wrote this while my Izzie (ten year old Jack Russell) was sitting by my side. Cancer took her too soon, and the hole in my heart will never be filled.

Murder most foul, as in the best it is.
But this most foul, strange and unnatural.

William Shakespeare (Hamlet)

Chapter One

"Vic! Where are you, hooker? I texted you so you could meet me outside!" My bestie with a chestie, Cory, bellowed from downstairs. I had seen his text but didn't respond. I wasn't ready, and you couldn't rush a queen getting ready to meet a bunch of other queens. We were on gay time, and that meant I'd be ready when I was ready.

"Almost done!" I called as I fixed my coif to perfection. Being a retired hairstylist meant I could work some hair, and my bangs looked like a fabulous wave perched on top of my head. I sprayed it so it would survive the day and turned my head to glance at the back. Fabulous, as always.

I grabbed my powder brush and quickly applied a light layer over my cover stick. Beating and patting until it disappeared, giving me the perfect complexion for meeting a group of harpies who came to fight for a crown.

Oh, I should explain that...

Hold on.

"Seriously, sister! If we don't leave now, we're gonna be late." Cory was pacing. He was always pacing when he was in a hurry, and he was always in a hurry whenever he came to pick me up. Yes – I was always late. I had a very busy life that came with three distinct personalities and disguises.

The basic me was a retired hairstylist that everyone in our sleepy little town knew. I loved a t-shirt or polo with a pair of slacks and a comfortable shoe, most of the time. This was what I called my boy drag because, as Ru always says, you're born nude but whatever we surround ourselves with is the drag we choose. And I love me some drag!

My second personality is Raven Ravonne, and she is sickening. Raven is the life of the party and the hostess with the mostess at the local gay bar called Rumors here in Maple Bay. I got my start in San Francisco, and when I moved here, I was hired immediately. Raven is my spirit animal, and I feel the most comfortable when I am wearing her. She takes no shit. Everyone loves her in town. I have hosted all kinds of events, and my drag persona is well known.

The third piece of drag that I slide over my own personality is more...complicated and secret. When I moved here to Maple Bay, I did something I had always wanted to do. I pursued a career as a writer. I've written my entire life but never had the guts to show it to anyone else. I threw a silly name on the book when I finished it – Vicki Dean. Lo and behold, much to my surprise, I got a phone call and couldn't believe my luck. I was going to be a published author. I told them about my ruse, and the publisher allowed me to continue it. I had so many fears. What if the reviews were awful? What if the public hated it? So, I kept Vicki, and she became a corporation and a kind of protection for me.

Everyone in Maple Bay thought Vicki a recluse, and she became an easy target for those with loose scruples. A few months ago, she... meaning I... was framed for the murder of the town's mayor. It was time for me to unleash Vicki upon the town, and she pursued her innocence with vigor. Cory, of course, was my partner in sleuthing, and somehow, lucky me, I met my boyfriend as he questioned me for the crime.

Sheriff Hottie, Harper Wolfe, and I have somehow managed my personalities, and he loves me no matter which of the three I am. He's open to all the possibilities, being a bisexual, and he loves me in boy drag or glamazon.

The murderers were discovered... Ok... Actually, they held me at gunpoint, and Cory saved my life. My secret remained a secret since they died while trying to escape. It was horrible. I knew them. I knew them very well, and it took me some time to deal with their betrayal and death. Only Cory and Harper knew my secret, and they were the only two people I trusted with it.

"I am serious, bitch! You need to move those skinny chicken legs downstairs right now!" I cringed. Making Cory, my assistant, seemed like a great idea at the time. He may look like a personal trainer, but he is the swishy sister of my soul. He's also a demanding bitch.

"Shut it, hunty! I'll be there in just a second."

"One! Well, that time has now passed. I think you like being late." I could hear his heavy sigh from the top of the stairs. Cory was nothing if not dramatic.

"Don't you throw shade at me. I said I'm coming!"

Now, where was I?

Oh, yeah. Harpies competing for a crown.

The Miss Gay Cali West Coast pageant was being held in our little town, and it was a big deal for Maple Bay. Rumors, our gay bar is a chain of sorts. There are eight other Rumors across America, and every one of them is privately owned and incredibly different. A friend of mine thought it would be the perfect place to host the pageant this year. She made some calls... and like seriously, she is a big deal in the drag world, and her calls can accomplish a lot. The next thing I knew, the bar manager was telling me about being chosen as the competition's host bar, and the town went wild with excitement.

What is both great and a little terrifying is I'm the emcee of the event. It's a lot of work and responsibility and will take up an entire week of my time. I am in the middle of edits on my next book, and my editor isn't happy with the delay, but it can't be helped. Have drag bag - must be fierce.

I walked down the stairs to find Cory, sure enough, wearing out my floor at the bottom of the stairs. He is breathtaking, and if he were anywhere else in the world, he would have an incredible boyfriend. His blonde hair makes him look like a surfer, with his bangs falling across his beautiful face. He stops pacing and glares at me with those deep blue eyes of his. Cory's body is a work of art since he is a personal trainer. He is corded with muscle and has wide shoulders and a narrow waist giving him the perfect V-shape.

Sounds butch, right?

Oh no... Cory is dressed in a pair of tight, light blue pants and a pink polo. His feet are adorned with pink, bedazzled rhinestone tennis shoes. He looks like a gay Dorothy just trying to get back to Kansas - Bless him. I worship him.

"Fierce." He appraises my outfit and coif. "Are you ready, boo?" He narrows his eyes and dares me to tell him, no. I nod and finish my descent, feeling like Scarlet O'Hara even though my staircase is very un-grand.

He hugs me and squishes me against his hard chest. My spine pops loudly, and I giggle. Cory gives fucking fantastic hugs.

"Come on, let's go or we're gonna be late," I chastise when he lets me go and brush past him as I head to the front door.

"Don't push it, ho. I'm nervous as shit." Cory shuts the front door behind him and locks it before we walk to his Prius. "We have a big day today, and with the registration of the contestants and rehearsing the opening number on top of all the other crap, I'm about to pop."

We crawled into the car, and I reached over and patted him on the leg.

"Child, we have planned everything, and it's going to go as smoothly as it can. Remember, we may be nervous about having to host the pageant, but the girls in it are going to be so tightly wound their wigs could pop at any moment. Just be nice and patient."

"Well, we can see how that's going, can't we?" He chuckled. "I almost came upstairs and carried you down."

We chatted about the edits on my book as we drove to the bar. My deadline was fast approaching, and I'd have to work hard after this pageant to finish them. Not to mention, I still hadn't written the ending. Cory was Vicki's assistant, as far as anyone in Maple Bay knew. He had been a giant fan and part-time stalker of her, so it made sense to bring him on part-time to help me out. Keeping my secret identity from him had been too hard, and telling him even harder. Cory, being Cory, didn't hold it against me. It was like he won the lottery when I finally told him under duress. He has been fantastic, and I haven't once regretted the decision.

Rumors was just a hop, skip, and a jump from my house. Literally, everything in Maple Bay was a quick trip since the town was so small. We parked in the back and walked in through the back door. Henry, the bartender, was setting up the small patio that they would use for service while the main bar was shut down for the pageant during the day. It wouldn't open until six every night. We would need every minute for rehearsals and time for the queens to work out their own talent routines.

"Hey, girls," Henry waved as we sashayed into the main room. "I set up the registration table in front of the stage for you. The branded table cloth looks like shit, though. It was a little too small, and I had to make it work."

"Thanks, Henry. We'll get the rest of everything set up. No worries. Has anyone from the pageant arrived yet?" Cory busied himself by grabbing some chairs for us to sit on while I opened my satchel and pulled out all the paperwork the pageant organizers had sent me. I placed the packets on the table and grabbed the pens I had brought, and placed them beside it. Each packet had the drag name of the contestant on it, so we could make sure there were no surprises. Drag queens were known to do whatever it took to win a crown, and I wanted to run a smooth pageant without any incidents.

"Nope. You're it," he answered as he started cutting

up fruit. "I got a late start this morning, so if you need anything, let me know. I'm just gonna stay out of everyone's way."

Cory and I futzed around getting everything as perfect as we could. Cory pulled the chairs down off the tables so they would all have a place to sit, and when we were done, we glanced around and liked what we saw. It looked organized and comfortable. Cory snapped his fingers and ran behind the bar and grabbed some small glasses and a few pitchers of water, and sat them to the side of the bar.

I flipped the light switch, and the bar's overhead lights flared to life. I walked behind the stage and flipped the stage lights on, dimming them to half. The giant banner for the pageant glowed at the back of the stage. The glitter on the crown sparkling with promise for all the contestants to see.

"Victor?" A deep male voice called as a tall thin man walked into the bar.

"Over here. You must be Joey." I stood and walked around the registration table where I had been sitting. "It's so nice to finally meet you."

"I know! We've talked so often; I feel like we're old friends." He walked over and totally invaded my personal space with a hug. I didn't mind. He was incredibly handsome. He let me go and turned to face Cory. "That must mean you are Cory. I've heard so much about you, but Vic never told me how handsome you were."

Cory literally leaped into his outstretched arms. I had to hide my smirk behind my hand. They might look like an adorable couple on paper, but two bottoms rarely find a way to make it work. I was a good judge of gay sexual hierarchies and rarely got it wrong. There was just something about the way a man stood that gave it away to me. I knew what Cory preferred, and Joey… Well, he called himself Joey. Bottom.

"It's nice to… uh… meet you, too," Cory said breathily, which made me have to swallow my giggle that threatened to erupt. It was cute. Joey was mid-thirties, handsome with a job, and lived out of town. He was perfect for Cory.

"The bar looks great, and it's much larger than I had guessed. The stage is perfect, too. All ten of the contestants will fit on it without a problem." Joey walked over to the stage and stared at the banner.

"Well, you can see that I rented an extension to the right and front of our normal stage. It expanded it another six feet in width and six feet in depth, which I knew we would need. I have everything ready, and the choreographer will be here at noon to begin the opening number for night one." I patted the stage, proud of what Cory and I were able to accomplish with the city's help. They gave us these extensions, and we didn't have to pay anything for them.

"Hey, ladies!" Henry stuck his head inside from the patio where he was setting up his bar. "You have a gaggle of gays out here, dying to get in."

I smiled excitedly and nodded at Cory.

"Open the gate and let the glamazon games begin."

I sat down beside Joey and took a deep breath. Here was hoping that everything would go smoothly.

Of course, it didn't.

"Did you have to hit me with your bag, you booger?" A loud, high-pitched voice asked shrilly.

"Sorry. I didn't see you there. Are you taller in heels? This isn't a Miss junior pageant, you know. Oh... Or a senior one." Oh, shit, these girls were already getting shady.

"You must need glasses, bitch."

"You must need directions to the lollipop guild, cow."

I started to stand, and Joey reached over and placed his hand on my shoulder. "This is nothing."

The girls started filing into the main room as soon as Cory opened the door. Each girl was accompanied by at least one other person. A couple of them seemed to have brought an entire team to the pageant. That was fine but not necessary for registration or the opening number rehearsal.

I glanced at all the bags they had brought with them and wondered where we were going to store everything. These drag-chicks did not come to play. A few of the contestants glared at one another, and the others seemed to not have a care in the world as if just being here was already winning for them. I knew that this was going to be dicey, but if I didn't say something quickly, it might turn into a fight scene from Showgirls in here.

"Can I have all the contestants... and the contestants only, please, in a line at the registration desk? Please have your ID and invitations from the pageant organizers ready to show. If you are not a contestant, please take a seat. For now." I said loudly, doing my best to be Raven even if I weren't actually wearing her today. I still needed her fire.

The girls all dug into their murses and pulled out the information I had asked for. Hopefully... Shady sisters like these were not known for following directions. They slowly started lining up at the desk. The first contestant looked like she had just smelled something especially bad. She slid her information over to me.

"Pam From Payroll." I read the name at the top of her letter. I grabbed her ID and double-checked the information we had. Shit. Pam's name was Melvin. I glanced up at her again and bit my bottom lip. She looked like a Melvin. "Welcome to Maple Bay. Have you checked into the hotel yet?"

"Nooo. I just got here," Pam snapped at me.

"I'm sure..." I stopped what I was doing and stared her down. This ho needed to know that I wasn't dealing with her piss poor attitude.

She fidgeted, and I knew – she knew, that she was about to get read for filth. "It was a long drive from San

Diego. Sorry. Carson wouldn't stop listening to Madonna... all the way up. I'm sure you understand."

"Madonna for nine hours? That's a bitch. How many people do you have with you?" I picked up her packet and handed it to her.

"I have five people. Two dancers and two stylists, and then Carson, of course. He's my drag sponsor. Are we going to be here all day, or will we get a break?"

"You'll have a break. We're doing the check-in and a quick talk before we adjourn for two hours, so you can check into your hotels. Then we come back and learn the choreography for the opening night number. There's a sheet in here for you to fill out, so we have the names of your backstage help and guestlist for the door. Make sure you turn that back in before you leave, please." I handed her back the ID and her invitation.

She walked over to her people and sat down before the next girl stepped forward.

"Hi. I'm Judy Ghouland." I took her information and gave her the same speech. She won the LA pageant, and that meant she had to be fierce. The girls there do not play. I had heard of her since she was a friend of my own special guest. She was polite and quick with a smile. I liked her instantly.

Our own local girl and a good friend of mine was next. Vivienne Westworld was a part of my cast here at Rumors, but she had won a pageant in central California to earn her spot here. She winked at me as I handed her the information. I did adore her, and she was classy as fuck.

"Did I hear that we're getting a break? I'm literally starving to death." A hefty redhead grinned happily at me.

"You did. Two hours and you are... Oh! Eatta Twinkie. I thought that was a cute name." I grabbed her ID and checked her in. "Do you have any guests?"

"Nope. Just me. I don't need a team of stylists to win. I can do that on my own." She said seriously, and I had to suppress my cackle. Coming by yourself to this large of a pageant was an admission that you had no idea what you were doing. Unless she was that badass. Usually, though, it just meant they were delusional.

"Well, there you go, hon. You checked in yet?"

"Yep. I've been here for two days already. It's a cute place. Thank you."

The next few girls were named Pussina, Dammit Janet, Shae Black, and Valerie Rage. They were all a little edgy, and I understood. The pressure would only grow on them as the pageant progressed. Three nights of competition was a lot, not to mention the three numbers they would have to learn quickly for each night's opening. It wasn't a sprint. It was a marathon, and some of these girls would not be ready. Drag roadkill was never pretty.

"Lil' Debbie." She slid her license in front of me with her letter and glanced over her shoulder to stare at someone while I checked her in.

"Do you have any guests?" I handed her back her information, and she snatched it off the table as if she were angry about something.

"What? Oh, yeah... My sponsor, Heather, will be here once the pageant starts, and I have my dancers and makeup guy with me. I heard I need to fill out the paperwork." She rolled her eyes and tapped her foot. This girl was not happy about something, and it was spilling over onto my day.

"Remember, this is supposed to be fun. Thank you, Lil' Debbie."

She huffed off and sat as far away from everyone else as she could. If she had people with her, she didn't choose to sit with them.

"Finally." The last contestant rolled her neck as if she would rather be anyplace else than here.

"Last but... not least?" I said snidely. This bitch was already on my nerves. I took her letter and let a laugh rip out. Her name was Karen. That was it, and it was perfect. "Would you like to file a complaint with the management? He's sitting right here, and I'm sure he doesn't give a shit." I tried a little humor. It bounced right off.

"I'm surprised the bar is so small. Aren't you expecting a large turnout? I mean, I know it's a small town and all, but... And is there a different hotel than the one the pageant chose? My room has this whiff of bullshit, and I didn't sleep at all last night." She came at me. Her rapid-fire feeling like little slaps across the face. I was about to stand up and let this ho have it when she grinned widely at me. "I like to stay in character."

"Bitch..." I said lowly. "I was about to pull out my can of whoop-ass."

"I'm method, I guess. It makes it easier. Drag isn't really my thing, just a means to an end."

"Well, let's save the acting for anyone but me. I have enough on my plate if you catch my drift."

"Sure. Sorry. It's just fun."

"If you have anyone with you..."

"I heard it all the other times." Karen rolled her eyes. "I'm alone."

"Ok. Have a seat then, hon" I sighed as I stared over at Joey. I wanted to say thanks for nothing, punk. He never said a word during the whole process. He just sat there on his cell phone, scrolling. Probably trolling on scruff. It was annoying. I would have rather had Cory sitting here beside me. He would have been helpful.

"Everyone signed in?" He glanced over at me, and I nodded. I should have taken the phone out of his hand and slapped across the face – thanks for the help, ho.

"Great." He grinned.

Joey stood up and walked to the back of the bar. He was not going to be any help at all. He, apparently, had something else on his mind. My dragtuition told me that Cory and I were going to have to do the heavy lifting if this pageant was going to run smoothly, all alone.

I stood up, and Cory, bless his heart, walked over and stood beside me.

"Alright, ladies. Today is going to be a long workday. You have the next two hours off, so you can grab some lunch and check into the hotels. I need everyone back here at two sharp, and please bring the heels you plan on wearing for the opening number. This is the California number. If your costume is difficult or you see any issues with moving in it, please bring that too."

The girls all stared at me blankly. Lord, have mercy. This was going to be an uphill climb.

"My name is Raven, and I am the emcee for the pageant. This is Cory, and he will be handling backstage for the show. Please leave the entourage at the hotel for all rehearsals that aren't your own. These are closed rehearsals, and that means no one, not even your sponsor, should be in this bar while we are working. There is a schedule in each of your folders, and I expect all of you to be on time. I will not put up with any diva shenanigans. I've been around for a while and have no shits left to give. Got me?"

I stared at them, and they nodded with various levels of excitement. A tall greasy looking man stood up and waved at me. Damn, he was kind of hot if you liked street trade. That t-shirt of his was so tight it might as well have been skin.

"Yes?" I gestured.

"I'm Domino, Ms. Pussina's sponsor. Will we be

able to attend our own girl's rehearsal? Her team and I would like to…"

"Yes. Of course, you can. Her time is her time, and that would include you, too."

"Thank you." He grinned at me and flashed a set of pearly whites so white they almost glimmered. He was a shark. I had heard tales of him from some of my friends still in San Francisco. He might be cute, but he was trouble.

"Any other questions?" I sighed.

"What about tech and pyrotechnics? Will that be a part of the rehearsal, or will there also be time with the tech director?" He spoke again and crossed his manly arms.

"It's all in the folder. You have two rehearsal slots and a tech slot the day before. I'm not sure that pyro is allowed in the bar, though."

"But we planned…"

"I'll have to get back to you on that, ok?" I cut him off. Sponsors were always going to be the difficulty with hosting a pageant. They paid and financed their contestant and made money on the national tour of the winner. Usually, they owned the bar that the queen called home. "Any more questions?"

"I have one." Another tall and skinny man asked from his seat. "I invest a lot of energy and expense into my contestants. I'm not a fan of this closed rehearsal thing. This didn't happen last year." His nasal voice was like a male Fran Drescher's.

"What's your name?" I smiled at him when what I wanted to do was throw something across the room and hit him in the head.

"I'm Carson DeVoor from San Diego, Pam From Payrolls' sponsor." He stared at me, trying to intimidate me into changing the rules.

"The pageant bylaws leave that up to the host bar, and that means me for this event. Learning these routines will be difficult enough without non-contestants chiming in, trying to get their contestant in the front and center. It will be equitable, and I am not changing my mind. You can explore the town during rehearsals." I answered, making sure there was no waver in my voice—what a dick.

No one said anything else, but Carson rolled his eyes and huffed in response. Domino just stood there and glanced around at the other girls as if he were searching for their weaknesses. Like I said, he was a shark.

"Great. I'll see you all at two." I glanced at all the bags lying on the floor. "Oh! Please only bring the costumes and clothes you will need for each night of the pageant. You know what happens to a girl's costume if it's left hanging around. We all got a pair of scissors, and it would suck if your gown got ruined. You all look like some catty bitches who want a crown." I laughed, and they all nodded. "See you all at two."

The girls stood up with their entourages and started grabbing their bags and walking to the front door. Two girls stood and stared at each other. Karen and Lil' Debbie looked like they were about to get in a catfight. They must have been the two girls bitching as they entered. Karen towered over Lil' Debbie, but if there was a fight, my money would be on her. She looked tough as nails. Karen turned and walked away, and Lil' Debbie glared daggers at her back.

"That ho's gonna get her wig snatched." She hissed at one of her large male dancers. He was standing in fourth position with his hand on his hip.

"Careful, sis." He glanced over at Cory and me before picking up one of her bags and hauling it over his shoulder. "Come on."

Lil' Debbie turned and stopped in her tracks as Pam From Payroll and her entourage walked by. Pam smiled at her, and Lil' Debbie glanced down at the floor. She adjusted her bag and followed behind. There must be some water under that bridge, baby.

I grabbed Cory's arm and waited until all the girls left before turning to him and grimacing. "This is gonna be a hell of a week."

"Sis, please. You want me to go grab some lunch for us or something." Cory glanced over at Joey, who was now leaning over the bar, still glaring at his phone. I saw what Cory was looking at, even if I did have to squint at Joey's flat ass. I elbowed Cory in the ribs and pursed my lips.

"Joey? You want to go with Cory and grab some lunch? I thought I would stay around here and wait for the choreographer. I think I should warn her what she's working with. Only a couple of these girls look like they can actually dance."

He turned and smiled at Cory. "They're better than they look. But lunch sounds great. Maybe you can show me around town later, too. I mean, I still need to check into the hotel myself."

"Oh, I'm sure Cory can help you with that too, Joey. You don't mind, do you, hon?" I smirked.

Cory's face was stoic. "It would be my pleasure."

They puttered around for a bit before heading out. I watched them sashay away and wondered how soon I would find them making out behind the curtain. Cory deserved someone who would make him feel like the amazing person he was. I would be keeping my eye on Joey. Hurt my sis, and I break your fucking face. I can get butch quick, or so I liked to believe.

Roy, the choreographer, showed up around one, and I gave him the down-low on the talent as I saw them. I warned him of their attitudes and the possible costume drama we might be in for. I was sure that someone would come as a fucking Golden Gate Bridge, and that could be a disaster for the other nine girls. Imagine being pushed off the stage or run over by a bridge in heels. Horrifying.

He showed me the number, and I was pleased that it was incredibly simple. With only a few hours to learn it and stage it, we were already pushing our luck. Roy was a pro, and I was lucky to have him. He and I had been friends for a while. He ran the dance studio here in town and was a big old sis. He could also outdrink anyone at Rumors. I had seen him shoot a bottle of tequila.

"The best has arrived!" Vivienne sashayed into the bar with a pair of heels and a large wig head. Sitting on it was a piece of wig art in the shape of a computer screen. She went all Silicon Valley for the challenge. Well, for Vivienne, maybe it was Silicone Valley. She was a filler queen whose lips were pumped, plump.

"Bitch, please. I'm half your age and twice as pretty." Shae Black entered behind her and slapped her on the ass. Vivienne seemed to like it. Shae was a pretty boy with a mane of red hair and a twinkle in his eye. I had seen his pictures on the internet when I researched all the contestants. He was beautiful in or out of drag. Apparently, he was also a cam model. I did fall down the rabbit hole with him. Sheriff Hottie was fascinated too. Who wouldn't be? He had a pole installed in his bedroom, and let's just say he's very flexible.

"I really needed that nap."

"I wish. I couldn't get the dancers out of my room. Thankfully Carson stayed in his own. After that car ride, I didn't want to listen to him."

Pam From Payroll and Judy Ghouland walked in together and took a seat. I guess they knew each other.

A few of the other girls walked in quietly and sat down in small groups. Everyone had a pair of heels in their hand except for Valerie Rage. She had red stiletto boots with what looked like a sickening eight-inch heel. Good for her. I would topple over.

"Is that everyone?" I counted and found I was missing two girls still. Eatta Twinkie and Lil' Debbie hadn't arrived yet. Maybe they were sharing gossip about yummy sugary goodness. "We'll wait for another five before we get started. I would suggest you stretch a little, ladies."

Some of the girls stood and started doing just that. Pam From Payroll and Karen just sat in their seats and scrolled through their phone.

"Sorry!" Eatta Twinkie ran into the room. "I got held up. The cops arrived at the hotel, and I had to wait for them to let us out."

"The cops?" Pussina asked as she bent down to touch her toes.

"At the Maple Bay Hotel?" Dammit Janet slowly slid down into the splits. "I didn't see anyone."

"No. A few of us are staying at the Beach View Motel. It was cheaper." Eatta gasped, shaken up at what she had experienced.

My cell phone vibrated, and I pulled it out. My boyfriend, Sheriff Harper Wolfe, was calling me. "One-second, girls."

I walked onto the patio, and I answered. "Hey, sexy."

"Vic... I've got some... Can you come down to the Beach View? I think... I think one of your queens from the pageant has been... She was found murdered in her room." His voice was husky. He was shaken up.

"What? How?"

"I think you should... We need someone to ID the body, Vic. Apparently, he checked in with a couple others, but they aren't in their rooms. There are wigs everywhere, so I assumed..."

I sat down because the patio started spinning. Murdered? Shit... I was still missing a girl. Lil' Debbie still hadn't arrived.

"How, Harper?"

"There's a stiletto buried a few inches into her head."

"Holy shit." I waved over at Henry, who immediately took a look at my face and poured me a drink.

Death by stiletto? What the actual fuck.

Chapter Two

"*That* was something I will never unsee." I wiped my eyes. I didn't know her, but she was still my sister, and dying that way... so violently... Her dancers came back to the hotel while I was there, and that was a whole lot of drama. I could tell that they loved her. Their grief was raw. Harper asked them to stay in town for a few days, and they agreed.

It was sad to see all of her gowns hanging forlornly on the small portable rack she brought with her. They looked super expensive, and I was impressed by the wardrobe she had unpacked. She would have done well in the pageant if she had been given a chance. That had been taken away from her. Who would do this? Why?

The department swept the room for any prints and discovered that the camera system at the hotel had stopped working a few weeks ago, and they hadn't gotten it fixed yet. Hopefully, they would find something. The other shoe was found on the floor, and her dancers said that the heels did belong to her. That murder was an act of hate. It had to be.

What was so bizarre was there didn't seem to be any struggle involved. That made no sense unless she knew the killer and trusted him. Possibly her... But why?

Would someone murder a queen just to win a crown?

I couldn't believe that. At least, I didn't want to.

"I... I won't either. A stiletto in the brain is... I mean, how did that even happen? The force you would..."

"Harper, can we not? Not right now," I asked quietly. This death hit too close to home for me.

"Do you need to go back to the bar?" He pulled me to him and held me close against his firm chest. The ink on his arms bright in the midday sun. I placed my face against him and breathed in the scent of my love. It brought some form of comfort to me. He smelled like sandalwood and man.

"No. Cory's there and is handling things. I'm... I'm going to have to tell the other girls, though."

"Not tonight. I want to get ahead of this as much as possible. If we can't find evidence that points a certain way... I'll need to question them." He let me go and tilted my chin up to him. "You going to be ok?"

"I'll have to be. I have too much to do to fall apart,

Harper." I ran my fingers through my hair, feeling my coif fall apart. "How long do you think you'll be? I can't go back there, I don't think. They're just learning the opening number today, and they have the night off, so... I think I'll go home."

"Good, babe. I don't know how long I'll... As soon as we're done here, I guess. The boys at state will start the lab work right away. I've already called them, and they're waiting for it. At least a few hours, I would guess." He bent down and kissed me, and it did make me feel better, but it couldn't cut through what I had seen.

I was numb. Shit... I was scared.

"I'll see you when you come home, then."

I called an Uber. Thankfully one was available, and I didn't have to wait long. There are only a few drivers in town. I texted Cory and told him to come to my house as soon as they were done. We had a lot to discuss, and even the thought about facing the other girls' tomorrow was turning my stomach. He, of course, wanted to know what was happening. I didn't want to tell him while he was there. If Cory knew – everyone would know. He had a shitty poker face.

I lay down on the couch and thought about every-thing I had seen today. Sure, the girls were catty. They had come to win the title, and that meant being aggres-sive and holding your own against the competition, but none of them were killers. If it wasn't one of them, then who? Lil' Debbie's dancers fell apart when they were told what had happened. It was too honest and real, but I had been fooled before, hadn't I?

Was this about the pageant, or was it something else altogether? Did she invite the wrong person inside her room? That would mean there was another killer running around town amongst us. But why her? That didn't make sense unless it was a drifter of some kind. Here in Maple Bay, a drifter would have been noticed, and the police would have been alerted. It's just the kind of town it was. But they knew the event was happening and there would be a lot of unknown people around. So, maybe?

Questions were all I had.

I had been here before, and I didn't like it. But this wasn't my mystery to solve. I had enough on my plate right now. The pageant and the edits to my book were going to take up all of my time, and even if they didn't, I wasn't a cop. Harper hated when I got involved in my own mystery while trying to clear my name. I reminded myself to stay in my own lane, but the wheels in my brain wouldn't stop turning.

I thought back to who she left the bar with. Her dancers were all that I remembered. There was that little kerfuffle with Karen, but she wasn't even staying in the same hotel. She had already checked in, though. All she had to do was go back to grab her shoes. She would have had plenty of time, but would Lil' Debbie even let her in the room? She didn't appear to like her very much... Was that feeling mutual? Seemed to be.

Besides, Karen was a little thing, and I couldn't believe she had the strength to get that heel... Jesus.

A crown and a chance to go to the national competition... Was that what her death had been about? She wasn't even expected to win. There were clear favorites, and as cute as Lil' Debbie may have been, she hadn't been one of them. Maybe someone knew something I didn't.

I closed my eyes and drifted off into a dreamless sleep.

I awoke to Cory and Harper speaking in hushed voices. They were sitting in the chairs that flanked my couch. I fluttered my eyes open, and the light was much softer than before. It had to be late afternoon.

"You don't have to whisper. I'm awake." My voice was hoarse. I woke up sounding like Bea Arthur and moving like an eighty-year-old who was crippled with arthritis. I blamed the heels.

"We were trying to be quiet," Cory said quietly. Harper must have told him; he was as white as a ghost.

"I needed to get up. How long have you been here?" I sat up. Bones cracked back into place as I stretched my arms and legs.

"Not long. Fifteen minutes or so." Harper stood up and came to sit beside me, taking my hand in his. "You ok, Vic?"

"No... I don't think I am. Why does this... Does it seem that this kind of stuff follows me around? I feel like a bad omen." I shook my head. It was more to shake the groggy from my brain than anything else. I felt like I had a hangover.

"Oh, Vic. It wasn't your fault, hon. All of the girls wondered, since she didn't show up if this meant that Lil' Debbie would be allowed to compete. I told them I didn't know anything and thank God I didn't. Joey does want you to call him, though." Cory looked like he was on the edge of panic. This was too much of a surprise. Murder always was, though.

"Have you heard from the lab yet?"

Harper nodded. "I got the prints back because it was so easy. The only prints in the room belonged to the cleaning woman and Mr. Barry Thompson. The real name of Lil' Debbie." He looked at me crestfallen. "I was really hoping there would be a print on the shoe. It was missing the rubber at the tip, so that's how it went in so far to the skull."

I grimaced. "That's unfortunate. So, with the lack of video surveillance and no prints, where does that leave you?"

"No eye-witnesses either. No one saw anything at the hotel, which sucks. The kid working the front desk had been watching a movie on Netflix. He saw nothing. But we did recover what might be a shoe print, maybe. We'll have to see. It was quite faint and may have belonged to the dancers or even Barry himself."

"How was the body found? The only people I saw with her were her dancers, and they weren't the ones who..."

"No. She had called about getting more towels, and the cleaning lady found her. Poor old lady. She said this was going to make her retire." Harper glanced over at me.

"So, no fingerprints... No bystanders that saw anything... No sign of a struggle... No clues except for the shoe being the murder weapon. Did you do toxicology? DNA?"

"Of course, and it's being rushed thanks to a friend of mine. We should get the results back tomorrow afternoon, but I don't expect to find anything that's going to help us unless there's some trace DNA evidence."

"Which only helps if we can get DNA samples from any of our suspects, which we can't legally do until we have something credible on them," Cory added and leaned forward on his chair, resting his elbows on his knees.

"How illegal would it be to get DNA samples and run them, just in case? It might point us in a direction..." The wheels were turning, and the glance that Harper gave me meant he knew. I was surprised that he didn't jump in and tell me that there was no we in the investigation. He sighed heavily and sat back on the couch.

"I think that I might need Vicki on this? The force wouldn't blink if Vicki was involved, but there's no way my boyfriend can help, even if he is the one running the pageant." He admitted and placed his hands in his lap.

"I'm sorry... Did you just ask for me to get involved in your case, Sheriff Hottie?" I said in mock surprise.

"Not you." He said pointedly. "Vicki. She can be anywhere and everywhere, and people wouldn't bat an eye. I know you have to do the pageant, but Vicki could drop by every so often, couldn't she? Maybe sit in on some interviews since you know more of what's going on at the pageant. Would you be able to handle that? I know nothing about drag queens except I'm dating one."

The way he looked at me made me feel needed. The sheriff's department would be in way over their head in dealing with drag queens. Hell, our vernacular alone could make people's heads spin. I nodded and grimaced.

"I don't know how I can handle being 2 people... well 3 people, easily for a week. I could let Cory handle the rehearsals, but I would still need help in dealing with everything else. It's not like Victor can just disappear during all of this. I have more than enough to deal with, but... How can I say no?" I shrugged, trying to find a path where Victor and Vicki could both exist over the next few days.

"What's the shortest amount of time it would take you to slide Vicki on?" Harper asked timidly.

"So no one has a chance of recognizing me as Vicki... At least an hour of beating my face. But I won't have that much time. I need to find a way to change into Vicki quicker than that. If I do no underpainting and only put on the lightest of makeup... Use a hat, maybe, so those dragons don't clock the wig... I'll figure it out, but if I have to disappear quickly and the pageant needs Victor, my absence will not go unnoticed. I think I'm gonna have to call in a favor."

"You don't mean?" Cory asked, almost bouncing out of his seat with excitement.

"She was going to be here for the three competition days anyway. What's a couple more? Besides, according to her, she has a nose for mystery." I grinned, thinking it through. "She would be a great go-between and could handle anything thrown at her."

"But wouldn't you have to tell her your secret?" Cory asked carefully.

"Who are you talking about?" Hudson finally interjected. He had been watching us like a tennis match.

"Ursula Moolay." I placed my hand on Harper's knee. "I think I can trust her. I don't see how I have any other choice."

We all stared at each other—no more words passed between us as they let me come to my own decision. Ursula wouldn't just be a big help to the pageant. She knew drag better than anyone and had been involved in solving quite a few mysteries of her own. Perhaps she could also help Harper if she agreed, whenever I couldn't be there?

I stood up and swiped my cell phone to open it. I pressed her number and put her on speakerphone.

"Hey, girl." Her deep contralto sounded lush and vibrant. "How's tricks, Trixie?"

"Ursula... I could really use... you... your help." My voice faltered.

"What's wrong, sis?"

I told her about Lil' Debbie, and she gasped. "My bags are already packed. I'll be there in the morning, boo. Someone messes with my sisters, and they don't just have you to answer to. Drag queen justice is about to be served."

Chapter Three

I had Vicki's bag packed and drove myself to my little cliffside ocean cottage. It was Vicki Dean's writing office, and I made sure to never go there as Victor. It would be hard to come up with a reasonable explanation as to why Victor Sommers was coming and going from Vicki's cottage. But I didn't see how it could be helped if I was going to assist with the investigation. Time management was going to be incredibly important.

I was also driving Vicki's car, but it's a gray Prius. There were a ton of Prius' in town, so maybe no one would notice. The problem was, most of the people in town were super nosy and paid attention to everything. It was one of the reasons I fit in so well here.

My secret identity was important to me, but it wasn't as important as finding Lil' Debbie's killer. I had come to peace with my decision. This was the only way for me to be of use to Harper. I spent the night beating my face and scrubbing it off repeatedly. I got my change over to Vicki in under thirty minutes which was about as good as it could get.

Would the other queens clock me? Would they see Victor under the makeup? Just in case, I brought a baseball hat to wear whenever Victor was around the girls. The more I could hide myself, the better it would be. My wig was real hair, and most of the time would be spent pulling my own through the lace-front so they wouldn't see the line of the wig. I had gotten good at this. Hopefully, it would be good enough.

I dropped off Vicki's things at the cottage and headed over to the bar. The girls were supposed to be there at eleven this morning to rehearse the opening and start learning the next routine. Then they each had 45 minutes to go over their own talent portion on the stage. That would give me enough time, I hoped, to complete my transition and return as a celebrity guest.

But first, I had to tell the girls about their sister. These pageant queens knew each other pretty well. Most of them traveled around until they won a qualifying pageant that would get them to the state level. It made them friends and sisters even if there was a competitiveness between them. They knew each other's journey as it was also their own. This would not be easy, and I already felt fragile.

I called Joey last night and told him the news. He took it hard. He had known Lil' Debbie, just as he knew all these girls since he oversaw all of the qualifiers as well as the state competition. His grief was palpable over the phone. The shock of the news making me worry about him and asking if he would like me to come to be with him, so he wasn't alone. He said no, thankfully. My nerves were already as thin as my pantyhose, and I really needed to buy new ones.

I parked in the back of Rumors and walked in to find Cory and my special guest chatting away. Well, Ursula was being peppered by questions from Cory about her reality show. He was a big fan. She looked gorgeous in a leopard print caftan and a pair of chunky boots. Her face was beat to the gods, and she was sporting a small afro that reminded me of those Foxy Brown movies. She was fierce as hell and knew it. That's how she survived all the tragedies that happened to her.

Ursula and I met for the first time while I was being investigated for murder. Of course, I never told her that. She came back a month later, and we spent a weekend getting to know each other better. Since then, we had become texting buddies and spoke on the phone every so often. It was with her recommendation that Rumors was chosen to host the state pageant this year. Ursula was supposed to serve as a judge, but with her new role, that would have to change. I think she was happy about that. She had recently confided to me how much she hated judging drag pageants. It made her feel like a villain to crush so many people's dreams. I knew what she meant.

"Biiiitch!" Ursula stood and strode over to me. The sound of her chunky heels echoing like gunshots across the concrete floor. "It's so good to see you." She held her arms open, and I fell into them. There was something about Ursula that made you feel safe. She was motherly and kind, and you knew that when she cared for you, it meant something important.

"Thank you, Urs." I smelled her perfume, and it smelled expensive. She had excellent taste.

"Oh, don't worry about it, child. I'd rather help you than sit behind a table. I'm just shocked that Lil' Debbie is... I mean... Death by a pump isn't something I would wish on my worst enemy. Damn... So, what can I do to help you, hon?" She brushed her red lips against my cheek, and I hugged her tighter. "Now, Vic, baby... It's gonna be ok."

I slowly pulled back and led her over to the bar. I nodded at Cory, and he hurried behind the counter and grabbed three glasses off the shelf.

"Bourbon and coke? Did I remember that correctly?" He picked up a bottle of KY Birddog and scooped some ice into the glasses.

"Oooh, girl. It's a little early for me..."

"Just this once. I have to tell you some things, and I think it will be better with some liquid courage." I placed my hand against hers on the bar, and she looked up at me with her big brown eyes and nodded slowly, waiting to hear what I had to say.

"I have to confess something to you, Urs. It's a secret that only two other people know, besides my agent and..."

"Your agent? I didn't know you were an actor, honey."

"He's not... Well, I guess he kind of is, actually." Cory poured the bourbon into the glasses with a flourish.

"Look at you, Cory!" Ursula cackled. "You're quite good at that, sunshine."

"Thanks, Ursula." He blushed.

"Call me Urs, honey. That's what momma's friends call her." She chuckled throatily, almost a purr. "Ok, spill the tea, baby. Momma can't stand secrets because she likes to be in the know, you know?"

"Do you like to read, Urs?" I cocked my head and watched her eyes narrow as she studied me.

"Sometimes. It depends on my mood. Why?" she asked as Cory poured some coke into the glasses.

"Have you ever heard of Vickie Dean?"

"The mystery author? Of course. I remember when we first met, there was a to-do around here about her." Her eyes opened wide, and she reached up and covered her mouth. "I remember Cory talking about her being a recluse and no one ever really seeing her in town... Hmm... I suppose there's a reason for that, huh?"

"I knew you would figure it out." I nodded. Cory scooted our glasses over to us, and Ursula took a large sip.

"Well, that's spilling the tea, baby." Ursula laughed.

"Sip, sip, bitch." I grinned.

"That's... something, Vic. I'm... honored that you told me, and I will keep your secret, but I'm not sure what this has to do with why I'm here. But I know it does, somehow, and that makes me a little uneasy," Ursula admitted frankly.

"Harper wants me to... Well, actually, he wants Vicki to help him with the investigation. At least whenever it comes to dealing with people from the pageant since I speak fluent drag." I took a sip and glanced up at her.

"I see." She sighed heavily, her ample bosom heaving. "He believes that someone involved with the pageant is the killer. It would be the obvious choice. It's the simplest common denominator." She took another slow sip and looked between us. "But I know most of these girls. A few of them I've known for a long time, and to think of any of them as killers... I can't believe it."

"I know. We may treat each other callously sometimes, but we are all sisters, and... It's just the only thing that makes sense. We're a small town that's incredibly liberal, and no one here would have any reason to kill someone... Well, some random drag queen in a hotel room with her own shoe. It has to be someone with ties to her in some way... It was personal the way she died, Urs. There was no struggle that could be found. It was like she knew her killer. Like she let that person in."

"I see... Damn. If one of these mother fuckers is a killer... If they would kill for a fucking crown and a stupid sash, then we have to get to the bottom of it. Your hottie hubby, Harper, is leading the investigation? Should I call Kris? He wouldn't have any jurisdiction here, but I'm sure he would be happy to help." Ursula batted her eyes at me. I could see that her eyes were misting over. This was personal.

"I think Harper has enough guys working the case in a legal procedural way, Urs. What he needs is someone who can talk to the queens and gain their trust. He needs someone who knows them and their ways. He can't really ask me to help with the investigation, but Vicki Dean has already helped the cops, and having a celebrity hanging around... Well, you know how queens are. They're gonna gag over you."

Ursula cracked her neck. "And you want me to keep the wheels on the ground for the pageant and poke around? I can do that. How are you going to handle this... disguise of yours? Girl, I'm discomboobulated even thinking of it. Vicki fucking Dean!"

"Oh, Vic has been making appearances as Vicki ever since she was framed for murder. The town loves her... now. She even does a spot on the radio once a month. A town book club that I helped organize for her. Trust me, her disguise would fool anyone." Cory chimed in, pouring more Coke into his glass. "I'm already tipsy."

"Do the girls know about Lil' Debbie?"

"No. I'm... I have to tell them today. We made sure her dancers were sequestered away from everyone else, so they wouldn't let it slip. Did you know her well? Lil' Debbie?" I asked carefully.

"Not well. I performed with her a couple of times. She's from Long Beach, and we LA girls don't hang out with them very much. No one wants to take the 405 anywhere. She was pretty good friends with Pam From Payroll, though, if I remember correctly. She's going to take the news hard."

"That's good to know. Did you know of anyone who disliked her?"

"I would think most everyone. Lil' Debbie was a bit of a... spitfire. She was one of those queens who didn't suffer fools very well. But I don't know anyone who had that kind of beef with her... Not the kind that commits murder, honey."

"Well, let's finish these drinks and hide the glasses before anyone else comes. They should arrive in about fifteen."

And arrive they did. They trickled through the door in gaggles of gays, three or four at a time. Their fun frolicking voices fell silent as soon as they entered the bar and saw us standing solemnly in front of the stage. They knew something was up, even if they didn't know what it was. They all sat close - even Karen, the last to arrive, stayed near the others.

"Ladies. Thank you for being on time. I don't think that I need to introduce the diva standing here beside me, as I'm sure you already recognize her. Ursula Moolay, at my request, will be helping me with the pageant, as my time has now been pulled in other directions. I'll still be here with you when I can. But I am pleased to know that you will be in excellent hands with Ursula and Cory."

"Hi ladies," Ursula purred, and the girls stared back at her, excitement obvious on their faces. Ursula was, after all, a celebrity. "I'm looking forward to working with all of you."

"I heard that the opening number was looking great after yesterday's rehearsal. But... I'm sure you noticed that one of the contestants was missing."

"Yeah. What happened to Lil' Debbie? Was she thrown out of the competition?" Shae Black asked, his red hair looking a little unkempt today.

"That is..." I cleared my throat. "I am sorry to inform you all, but Lil' Debbie was found murdered in her hotel room yesterday." Hands shot up in the air, and the queens started murmuring to each other. A palpable fear permeated the room. Not one of them looked like they were feigning surprise. It floored them and scared them to death.

"I can't really answer any questions, ladies. I'm not a cop, but I know that the sheriff's department will want to speak to each of you and any of your team that was in town yesterday."

"Why? They can't believe that one of us..."

"Girls!" Ursula clapped her large hands together loudly. "She done said she don't know. Of course, the cops want to talk to you. One of our sisters was murdered. I expect you to offer any information you have when it's your turn, and if you think you know something, please talk to Raven before we start rehearsal. Got it?"

The girls all nodded. Ursula was pure diva, and the girls listened. Thankfully...

"Do they think we're in danger?" Valerie Rage asked meekly. The color had drained out of her face, and she looked like she may throw up.

"Not that we know of. But I would be careful if I was you because we truly know nothing, as of now." Cory answered quickly, and I shot him a quick look. He threw his hand over his mouth.

"That don't sound like we're safe!" Eatta Twinkie's hands were fluttering all over the place.

"I know. I guess... I mean, Cory is right, I guess. Until we know something more... You're safer staying with others and not alone, I guess. Honestly, it's an open investigation, and I only know so much. Remember ladies, I am not a cop." My shoulders slumped, and Ursula put her arm around me.

"It's been a long night for sweet Raven here. But the show must go on, and one of you will be crowned Miss

Cali West Coast. So, pull yourselves together and take ten to put your heels on and check your fear at the door. Joey!" Raven exclaimed as the pageant coordinator walked through the front door, looking like he hadn't slept all night. Harper had spoken to him after the rehearsal last night, and Joey had taken it quite hard. He was friendly with all these girls since he ran the entire pageant system in California. They were his friends, and he was taking it hard.

"Ursula, darling! You got here early." He walked through the contestants who had spread out around the bar and began stretching.

"I thought Raven could use an extra hand with everything going on. We're gonna tag team the pageant, and I have another special guest arriving to take my place on the judge's panel. This way I'll even get to perform a number with Ms. Raven over there. Take the win, Joey. You holding up, honey?"

"I suppose. Did you already tell them the news?" He whispered to me, and Raven slipped her arm back around me.

"Yeah, she did, boo. They took it quite hard. The sheriff's office will want to talk to the girls today in between their talent rehearsals. Raven is going to find out the schedule and give it to me. She will be coordinating with the police department, and I will be making these bitches crown worthy."

"Sounds great. I'll just be sitting back here at the table coordinating with our PR rep about this incident." Joey sighed and walked over to a table in the corner of the bar.

"Joey needs to learn there's no such thing as bad press. I should know." Ursula chuckled. "Don't you have somewhere to be? Just text me the info, and I'll make sure to give the girls their time for the hot seat."

"I have an hour before I need to leave, actually. Thank you so much, Urs. You really are a lifesaver."

"Child... I love a mystery, and it usually almost gets me killed every time, but I can't stop myself." She turned towards the figure walking through the front door. Roy, our choreographer, was making his way towards us. I informed him of the situation and introduced him to Ursula, whom he was already a fan of because of her reality TV show.

"Girls. Get your shit together, and let's run through the opening with Roy. I hope you remember this shit because momma has not had enough coffee to be nice." Ursula barked, and the girls all ran up towards the stage.

They were a mess. The opening number looked like they had never rehearsed it, and Roy went over it slowly with them again. Ursula, Cory, and I sat at a table judging them and gossiping about anything else besides what was currently happening.

"Are any of you a dancer?" Roy huffed as he stomped his foot.

Valerie Rage raised her hand, and Roy rolled his eyes.

"Girl, you can put your hand down. Ok, let's go over this one more time, and then we really have to move on. You do know that the judges will be watching this, and it will influence their decisions, don't you?" Roy looked over to us for validation, and we all nodded.

"If you look like a fool here, it's going to be a long road for you." Ursula sighed, looking like she was annoyed by all of them. "Seriously! You hagathas need to get your shit together. You're looking more like Ms. Kentucky than Ms. Cali, if you get my drift."

"She knows. She's from Kentucky," Cory agreed, shaking his head enthusiastically.

"And I'm fabulous! Now show me why you're fabulous. Work that stage like you work the corner. Own it." Ursula demanded, standing up and walking over to the edge of the stage. "I've seen you all perform, and you are each unique and amazing. That's why you're here. Now show us why you deserve that crown."

They ran through the number again, and they were better. Ursula and Roy put them through their paces, and I watched them, studying them for something I wasn't even sure I understood. Could one of these queens be a good enough actress to hide the fact that they killed their competition? Watching them dance was murder enough.

"Take ten ladies," Roy said after he was happy enough to move on to the next number. "I do not want to have to go over this routine ever again. We have to start learning the second-night opening, and it's harder than this one, so be ready."

"There's a pitcher of water in the back - If you don't have your own." Cory rolled his eyes and pulled out his phone.

A couple of the girls walked to the bar and poured themselves a cup. Most of the other girls had their own water bottles with them. Valerie Rage sat down on the side of the stage and crossed her legs.

"Having someone like you here is really an honor. You're one of the reasons I became a drag queen." She smiled at Ursula, who walked over and stood in front of her.

"Is that right?"

"Yeah, watching you on TV really opened my eyes to what it was I wanted for myself. I've been thinking a lot about identity lately, and I feel... Oh my God!" Valerie stood and pointed to the back of the bar.

We all turned, just as the sound of what was happening assailed our ears. Shae Black and Dammit Janet were bent over and puking all over the floor. The sound was... I will never forget it. The worst stomach flu in the world was nothing compared to this. It was also not stopping.

Ursula and I glanced at each other, and both of us slowly walked towards them. When we got a few feet away, both of us gasped at what we saw.

"What the fuck! Did they eat a smurf?" Ursula said

slowly, afraid to get any closer. Blue vomit covered the floor.

"I'm calling nine-one-one!" Cory screamed.

I called Sheriff Hottie. This was not natural.

All I wondered is if the killer had struck again.

Chapter Four

"Copper what?" Ursula's eyes grew big as she tried to take in what was being told to us.

"Sulfate. It's used in gardening. The pitcher of water was tainted with it. Who sat the water out?" Harper looked tired. He and his detectives had made the girls leave everything here in the bar and patted them down to see if they had anything on them. Every girl was cleared and sent back to their hotel rooms. Nothing was found in their bags.

"So they were poisoned... That's a totally different MO than before. Whoever put that in the water had no idea who would actually drink it. It could have been anyone." I surmised slowly, letting this change to the killer's attack play in my mind.

"It could have been us? Or Joey. Have we heard anything from him?" Ursula sat down on the edge of the stage. She was wondering what the hell she volunteered for. I didn't blame her.

"Yeah, he texted a minute ago. Both of the girls are going to be fine and will be released from the hospital later today after they check their kidneys for damage. He's staying there with them, bless his heart. The doctors think they will be able to return tomorrow. They've flushed their system and seem to be doing fine." I answered.

"They were lucky." Harper's sharp retort was true. "Who placed the water?"

"I did. I pulled it from the tap and used the ice in the chest behind the bar." Cory looked as if all the color had drained from his face. "But I didn't..."

"I know, Cory." Harper stood and walked behind the bar, talking to one of his guys. We all watched as they opened the ice chest and placed a small piece in the beaker the detective had. He did the same with the tap water. He shook his head, and we all let out a collective sigh.

"So it happened after Cory sat the water on the bar. Did any of you see who came back this way after the water was placed?" Harper sighed, already knowing we couldn't answer his question.

"It could have been anyone. The girls were stretching all over the place. We weren't paying attention to... I mean, this is a totally different thing than Lil' Debbie's murder. That was focused, and this was... chance. Could it even be the same person who did it? I think we have to look at that possibility, don't we?" This was too haphazard. It didn't have a particular victim in mind because how would the person know who would be drinking that water?

"Well, the one thing they have in common is the pageant?" Ursula stared at me. "Someone was willing to take a chance on the lives of the other contestants for them to win the crown. That seems obvious to me."

"But is it really connected, or was someone just trying to... I mean, they didn't know about Lil' Debbie until we started rehearsing. That would mean they came prepared to do this anyway. If it was connected, that makes Lil' Debbie's murder even more personal, doesn't it? If the goal is to cut girls out of competing, so they have a better chance at winning... Why kill her at all? It just doesn't seem right." I stood up and walked over to sit beside Ursula. I grasped her hand and squeezed it. "What do we do? Cancel the pageant?"

"You can't. It's our best chance at finding the person who did this. Vic? I think it's time..." Harper winked at me.

"That means the show must go on, then. Hopefully, there are enough girls still standing to have a pageant." Cory looked grim. "Harper? Would that copper stuff have killed them, or would it just have made them sick?"

"It could have done either, actually. It depends on how much they ingested. It's water-soluble, according to Jack over there, and usually makes them sick upon hitting the stomach lining. But not always. Sometimes it just eats the body from the inside." Harper sat back down in our small circle.

"So, this is what we know already. Lil' Debbie was chosen as the first victim for a reason. It has to be more personal than the others. Anyone could be a victim if he or she was willing to let anyone drink that water. That means we could have a killer who is using any means necessary to achieve their goal, whatever that is."

"From a stiletto in the brain to poisoning is a wide range. Are we sure that it's even the same killer?" Ursula asked and looked over to Harper.

"No. We don't know for sure. But two incidents in less than twenty-four hours would be a surprising coincidence if it's not." Harper stood back up. "You can bring the girls back. We should also continue down the chosen path, Vic. Maybe we can learn something if we interview them one at a time. Can we still use the dressing room?"

"Sure." I agreed. "I won't be here for the rest of the day if you think that's ok. I've got something I need to do today." I said loud enough for the other cops to hear. They knew Vicki and me, so I wanted to give myself a clear path out of their view.

"No problem. I have a special guest coming to talk to the girls, anyway." He winked.

It was time to find out everything we could.

These girls were about to meet Vicki Dean.

Chapter Five

I walked into Rumors on the arm of Sheriff Harper Wolfe. Karen was up on the stage, working through her talent number for the competition. Good God... She had remixed Karen YouTube videos together into a dance song. I had to give her points for staying on brand. She watched me walk in, and I noticed her giving my boyfriend the old up and down with her gaze. I couldn't blame her for that either. I didn't call Harper, Sheriff Hottie, for nothing.

He led me over to Ursula and Cory, who were going to be bringing the girls in one by one for us to speak to.

"Ursula, I would like you to meet Vicki Dean." Cory grinned, a gleam in his eye. He loved our subterfuge more than I did.

"It's a pleasure to meet you, Ms. Dean. I'm a big fan." Ursula winked.

"Vicki Dean!" Karen screamed. "Oh, My God! I am

like… your biggest fan." She almost fell off the stage but recovered at the last minute, feeling foolish.

"Thank you." I smiled at her and noticed her blush. She really was a fan, maybe.

"Everything is set for you in the dressing room. I have fresh bottled water in a cooler for you." Cory wanted to make sure no one could tamper with them.

"Sounds lovely. Has the first person arrived yet?" I said tersely. I needed these girls to be off-kilter if I was going to find out anything about them, and that meant I couldn't think of them as my sisters any longer. They were suspects.

"Yes. I'll bring Pam From Payroll in whenever you're ready. She's sitting outside on the patio so she couldn't see the other contestant's talent." Ursula slid her hand against my arm and led me towards the dressing room. "Girl, I would never know. You are the fishiest thing I've ever seen. I am gagging over your eleganza. Best selling author realness, lady."

I giggled and smirked over at her before she let go and walked back to the main bar.

Harper and I closed the door behind us, and I took a seat in what was my usual chair. Harper pulled another chair beside me and placed the third in front of us a couple feet away. This would have been easier if we could have done this at the Sheriff's station, but that would make it seem that these girls were guilty, and we didn't know that yet.

A small knock sounded on the door, and Harper slowly opened it. "Pam From Payroll?"

"That's me. My real name is Melvin if you need to know that." Harper stood aside, and Melvin stepped in. He was wearing a t-shirt and jeans and had his hair pulled back in a ponytail. It was not unbecoming on him. This easy streetwear he was sporting made him seem more relaxed.

"Take a seat, Melvin. We just want to ask you a few questions. Thank you for agreeing to meet with us. This is Ms. Vicki Dean and..."

"The writer? Wow... What are you doing here?" He looked at me, confused. "I've read all three of your books. I love a good murder mystery. Of course, I wasn't planning on living in one."

"Thank you. Would you prefer us to call you Melvin or Pam?" I wanted him to feel safe. If he let his guard down, we may learn something useful to the case.

"I mean, I'm not in drag, so... Melvin is fine. I don't get it twisted." He touched the chair in front of me. "Is this where I should sit, Sheriff?"

"Yes, please." Harper took a deep breath, and his muscular chest heaved before he let it out. He knew how to play to his strengths too. "Melvin, you're from..." He glanced at the information I had supplied him.

"San Diego... Well, actually, Oceanside. It's where Denice Richards is from." Melvin talked with his hands, and they fluttered up in the air. "Sorry. I'm just a little nervous."

"We just need to ask everyone some questions, Melvin." I laid it on thick.

"No, not about this, really. I'm more nervous that I might be next, you know? I was runner-up last year, and I really think that this could be my year, but it seems like the girls are dropping like flies. It's... I feel like I have a target on my back, I guess. Well, me and Judy Ghouland. I think we are expected to be the top two this year." Melvin noticed his hands flying all over and placed them under his legs. "At least that is what my sponsor thinks and the rest of the pageant world, but you never really know. Sometimes a new person can come in and shake everything up."

"Your sponsor? Can you explain what it is that a sponsor does, Melvin?" I asked.

"Sure. I would think it's a lot like you having an agent, Ms. Dean. My sponsor pays for all of my pageant expenses. He hires and pays for the choreographer and dancers, travel, my outfits for the competition, and all of our food and drinks while we are here."

"Interesting. How many pageants do you go to in a year?" Harper asked as if he were really curious.

"I went to three other pageants this year. It helps to get us ready for the big one, and of course, I had to win one of the regional titles to compete in the state competition. I was runner-up in Ms. Los Angeles, but that was expected. Judy Ghouland's won that title for the last three years, and it was her home competition. I won Ms. San Diego, which I have also won for the last few years."

"Do you know all of the other girls?"

He made a funny face while he thought about my question, which was a little odd. It wasn't a hard question.

"I mean... Know... know? Then not really. If you mean, have I competed against most of them in the past, then yes. I'm friendly with a few of them, but outside of drag, I don't really know most of them. Does that make sense? I guess it would be like you and Stephen King at the same book fair. You may meet, but do you really know him?"

"Sure. That makes sense. Did you know Lil' Debbie... uh... Barry DeKalb?"

He sighed, and Harper leaned forward, placing his elbows on his knees.

"Yeah. I knew Barry. Not really well, but I performed in Long Beach sometimes at the bar he worked at. He was... Barry wasn't a very easy person to get to know."

"Meaning?" I pushed gently.

"He wasn't the friendliest of people. He was always kind of quiet until he got onstage. The last few times I worked there, he was a little nicer. Of course, he was usually a little tipsy at the bar. Most of us are when we're performing. I mean, it's a bar. But the last state pageant, he and I barely talked. He kept to himself and was kind of pissed when he didn't make the top three. I think he would have been in the running this year, though. I saw his talent at Ms. Los Angeles, and it was pretty fantastic. I thought it was so good that I insisted on changing my own to compete. I still... I mean, he never really tried to be my friend, but he was still one of us. I just can't believe that... Come on... murder? What the fuck?"

"It says here that you came with a group of five other people. Are you all staying in the same hotel?"

"Yeah, The Maple Bay Hotel. It's actually quite nice. We usually stay in dumps by the interstate to save money for sequins. This is a nice change."

"You have two dancers, two stylists, and Carson DeVoor, your sponsor, right? Would any of them have known Barry?" Harper asked quickly.

"No, I don't think so. One of my stylists knows Valerie Rage, but none of them ever mentioned Lil' Debbie. Carson knew her, of course. He knows every-one. The drag world, when it comes to pageants, is actually very small."

"One last question, Melvin. Did you see anyone near the water this morning before anyone drank it?" Harper stared him down, but I could already see that Melvin knew nothing.

"No. I'm just glad that I brought my own bottled water. The Beach View had them sitting out at their continental breakfast, so us girls grabbed a couple. I even gave Judy one of my waters, or she might have drunk from the pitcher too." Melvin narrowed his eyes. "Can I ask a question? Do you think that it's one of us? I can't... I can't believe that."

"Honestly, Melvin... We don't know. I think that's it for now." Harper stood, and Melvin jumped up too. I crossed my legs and frowned. This was what I expected. Did I learn anything? Carson was someone we should speak to, especially since he was staying in the same hotel as Lil' Debbie. But like Melvin said, all of the sponsors knew all of the girls.

"Thank you, Ms. Dean. It really was an honor to talk to you."

"Thank you, Melvin, and good luck with the pageant."

Judy Ghouland came in next, and she was not much help. She knew Lil' Debbie, of course, but just like Pam From Payroll, not very well.

"Barry was a perfectionist and pushed himself and his team really hard. Winning was important to him, and he never took losing very well. His dancers and sponsor lived in fear, I think, whenever they performed. Barry didn't like mistakes."

Judy also didn't see anything that morning. "Dancing is not my forte. I'm a comedy queen with two left feet. The only thing I was focusing on was trying to remember the choreography, so Ursula wouldn't scream at me again. If Pam hadn't given me that water... I would have drunk from it, too. Are they going to be coming back to the pageant? It's so horrible to work as hard as they have and not get to compete. Shae Black's talent number is maybe one of the best ones." Judy looked like she was about to cry.

"We'll have to see what the doctor says, but it looks like they will be able to return. Ursula and Raven are being kept up to date on their condition." I answered and glanced over at Harper. He heard it too. Shae would have been a strong competitor, at least in Judy's mind. Maybe the other girl's too.

Pam thought that Lil' Debbie had a good shot at placing this year. Judy thought Shae had an amazing talent portion to the pageant. Maybe this wasn't as random as we thought. Also, Lil' Debbie's team wasn't very fond of her, according to Judy. That didn't really jell with how they reacted when they were told of her death. They also had an alibi during the time of her murder. They were being loud and eating at The Bistro, so they couldn't have done it. But her sponsor? Was he even here? Why would he kill someone who he had put so much time and money into?

None of that felt like a path worth pursuing, but we had very little to work with, as it was.

Vivienne came in next. She was from here, and this was her first year in the Ms. Cali West Coast pageant. She usually competed in a different pageant system called The Entertainer. She knew almost none of these girls except for Shae Black and Pussina since they were from the San Fran area. She looked like she was re-thinking her choice of being involved at all. I didn't blame her. Vivienne was a quiet drag queen who worked part-time in the school with the after-school theatre program. I knew her well.

Pussina was new. I didn't really know her, as much as I had heard of her. She came out after I left San Francisco and worked in the show at The Brass Monkey with a couple of my friends. They didn't like her very much. But in Pussina's defense, my friends hated all the pageant girls.

That was a real thing in the drag world. Quite a few drag queens thought the pageant system was idiotic, and so were the girls who pursued a crown. The pageant girls thumbed their nose at the bar queens who just wanted to entertain. It was like West Side Story but with wigs. It was a vicious circle older than time itself. I had never been into pageants. They were too much work.

"So you knew Lil' Debbie?" Harper placed his hands on his knees and gave Pussina his million-dollar smile.

"Mmm-Hmm... I did. We've been talking on the phone quite a bit. She was thinking of moving to San Francisco, and I was helping her in whatever way I could. Bless her heart. She had really been through it recently. Poor thing."

"She was moving? No one else had mentioned that." Harper took a slow deep breath as he thought about this new piece of information.

"Mmm... I'm not sure who all knew about it, to be

honest. She was waiting to make the final decision until after the pageant." Her hands shook a little, and she placed them in her lap. "Sorry. I'm a little scared. This has been... it's a lot. I can't believe that bitch is dead. She was hella talented even if she was a little scary."

"I'm sure, hon. Murder is supposed to scare you." I added. "If Bar... Lil' Debbie was moving from Long Beach to San Francisco... What was she going to do with her sponsorship? I think her home bar was her sponsor. How would that work?"

"I mean... I guess she would have... Mmm... Yeah. She was looking for a new sponsor, actually. I know that she spoke to mine. He works with a few different girls, and I know that Domino spoke to her about joining his stable."

"Stable? That's a weird word to use." Harper glanced over at me.

"Mmm... Yeah. It just means that we all work under the same sponsor and use the same support team to help us. Right now, I am the main girl for this pageant system, but there are a couple others ready to take my place. One day, I'm sure, they will start placing above me, and then they will be the main girl. You get me?"

Harper nodded. "Not really. But I understand enough. Vicki here is a big fan of drag queens, though."

"Yes. So, if she was looking to change cities and sponsors... How often is that done? I would think that her current bar would not look kindly on her defecting. Do you know if her sponsor knew?" I asked carefully.

"I don't know. It's a very small world, and gossip travels fast. I'm sure you understand that." She shrugged. "Mmm... I just don't know who else she told. Lil' Debbie wasn't the friendliest of queens, you see. Most people didn't like her. I know that she didn't get along very well with the other girls at the competitions. She'd always been nice to me, though." Pussina looked like she was about to burst into tears.

"Did you talk to her after you arrived at the pageant?" I had wondered this. Maybe she had some information that could prove helpful even if she didn't know it.

"Just for a second while we were all walking to the hotel. But when we started checking in, she stayed with her people."

"Her dancers?" I asked, leaning forward and taking my glasses off.

"Mmm... Yeah. But there were a couple others too. I'm not sure who they were, though." She shrugged. "It was two other men. Both of them were tall and thin, but I didn't know them or really pay much attention."

"Pussina, can I ask you a question about the pageant system?" I feigned ignorance. "I've always found it fascinating. You are from San Francisco like Shae Black. Are you in the same... stable? I mean, does your sponsor take care of all the San Fran girls?"

"No. Shae is great, though. I really hope she gets better and can compete. We're really friendly even though she's a showgirl at a different bar. We still hang out every now and then since we're both fairly new. But Domino tried to get her to join us. He really likes her, but she's been with this new sponsor that I don't really know much about. She's this lesbian from Oakland, and Shae adores her." She looked around the room as if someone might have heard her. "Domino was really disappointed that she wouldn't let him groom her. I know Shae's sponsor isn't here yet. She was coming up when the pageant began. Does that help?"

"Immensely. Thank you, Pussina."

Eatta Twinkie was next, and he was completely useless. He knew almost nothing about the pageant circuit besides the one contest he surprisingly won. Being from Bakersfield and away from almost all the other girls, the only thing he knew was that he knew nothing. Honestly, Clinton, which was his given name, was incredibly full of himself. I could see why the other girls rolled their eyes around her. She didn't really want to belong with them.

The last contestant was Karen, who I remembered had come to the competition alone, like Eatta Twinkie. I also suddenly remembered the small confrontation that she had with Lil' Debbie at our check-in.

"Karen, I see that your real name is Benjamin Bradford, the Third?" Harper stated simply. He sat back in his chair and crossed his arms. His thick biceps and forearms flexing with the movement, I couldn't help but notice. It was distracting. Benjamin didn't even look at it, though. That was interesting.

"Pretentious, isn't it? My family is full of it." He sighed.

"How long have you been in the drag world, Benjamin?" I asked, actually curious. After our first conversation where he said drag wasn't really his thing, I wanted to know.

"Do you mind calling me Karen? I'm trying to stay in character, you see. I'm very method." He frowned and crossed his legs slowly as if he were Sharon Stone in Basic Instinct.

"Sure. You can be whomever you want, Karen. So how long?" I smiled tersely. This ho was already on my nerves, and we had just begun.

"I've been doing drag professionally for two years. But I started doing drag on Instagram first. I have a shit ton of followers, even if I'm from a small town in the desert. Have you ever heard of Barstow?" He looked at me sullenly.

"Of course, I have. So, you're from Barstow. Do you perform in a local club there?"

"When they let me. It's a gay country bar, and I'm the only drag queen. I perform once a month there on Wednesday nights. Sometimes it's just me, the bartender, and about ten people." He shrugged. "But it's still a chance to be onstage."

"That's tough. How did you get into the pageant

scene?" Now I really was curious. There had to be more to Benjamin Bradford, the Third than he wanted the world to see. He had the tenacity to get as far as he did. His shtick was clever and timely. I'll give him that.

"Barstow is as close to Vegas as it is to LA. So I signed up for a pageant in Vegas on a whim. I was horrible, but I found myself feeling more alive there than I did back home, so I signed up for another in Palm Springs. I lost there too. But this year, I won and didn't even realize it meant I would go to a state pageant. I've worked and scraped together every penny for this. All the costumes and wigs... Well, I make most of my own, but I bought an evening gown that's going to surprise the other girls. I love it." His face lit up as he told us about his journey. I found myself wishing I could help him in some way. The little fucker had gotten under my motherly skin.

"That's a great story. So many of the other girls have teams that help them prepare," Harper interjected, and I knew he felt the same way I did. One day, Harper and I would be great parents. Don't tell him I said that.

"Yeah, whatever. I don't need all that. I think of drag as acting, and I might not win this competition... Hell, I'm sure I won't. But I bet I have more fun than the other girls, and who knows, maybe next year?"

"Maybe... You have a great story, Karen." I smiled.

"I really am a giant fan, Ms. Dean. I paid for a pass to the San Francisco book fair a couple months ago to finally hear you talk about your books. There were so many rumors about you on the internet, you know, being a recluse and not feeling like you could go out in public... It was very exciting."

"Well, I hope you feel I was worth the price of admission." I laughed with my most feminine laugh.

"Oh, well worth it. When is the new book coming out?"

I stuck my finger against my lips. "At the end of the year, if I get these damned edits done, Karen. I think you'll like it. It's about a serial killer who develops an attraction to a writer, and... well, I really can't tell you more."

"Ladies. If we can stay focused, please." Harper chuckled easily.

"Karen. There were a few witnesses to an incident between you and Lil' Debbie on the day of registration. Would you tell me about that?" I asked as politely as I could, hoping to keep the camaraderie we had developed.

"Sure. She ran into my bag on the way in and rolled her eyes at me like it was my fault. I was just waiting my turn to go through the door. She was not very nice. I mean... I know she's dead, but... She was kind of a bitch." Karen uncrossed her legs and re-crossed them the other way, a frown firmly in place.

"I see. Had you ever met her before that?"

"Ms. Dean, I hadn't met anyone before this. None of these girls were in my regional pageant. It was the last one of the season, and they had all already won their titles. The only person here that I've ever met before was that guy Joey from the pageant. I'm a true lone wolf." Karen grinned, and it was a little alarming. Too forced. It made me shiver.

"Alright. I guess that's all I have, Karen. Do you have anything to add, Sheriff Wolfe?" I reached over and placed my hand on his arm.

"Out of curiosity, did you see anyone near the water during rehearsals?" Harper asked quickly.

"Sure. A lot of people when we were all walking around. Hell, I was over there. But I didn't see anyone... you know... Put anything in it. But I did see someone take a drink. Yes... Now that I think about it, Joey poured himself a glass before we started rehearsing. But he didn't get sick, so it had to be after that somehow."

"Are you sure of that?" I asked way too excitedly. "That would mean that the water was poisoned after rehearsals began. The only people not on stage were Victor, Ursula, and Cory."

"Yes. I'm positive. But I have to say, I never really looked over there again. Anyone could have come in, and I don't think I would have noticed because I was concentrating so hard on the choreography. We all were."

"That's all, Karen. Thank you."

She walked out of the room, and I stared at Harper, who looked at me as if he knew what I was thinking.

"The three of us were together the whole time. I know it wasn't any of them. Someone else had to sneak in here, and none of us noticed, Harper. How could that have happened?"

This case was proving to have more questions than answers. But three girls had been attacked. Would we find who the culprit was, or would there be more victims?

Chapter Six

$\mathscr{U}$rsula sipped her cocktail as she sat on my couch. It was nice to have her as a house-guest, especially with all of this happening. It took my mind off of the horrid events. She had taken off her makeup and wrapped a frilly pink robe around her adorable Power Puff Girls pajamas. They even had feet. Yeah, I was jealous.

Cory paced around the living room with his high-ball glass of gin and juice, threatening to splash out with every turn he made on my rug. Honestly, he was going to wear a hole in my floor if I didn't make him sit down. I was just too tired to say anything.

I had gotten out of drag, for the most part. Vicki's wig sat on its form, and I had changed into my favorite t-shirt and sweatpants, but I was still sporting the makeup. The thought of wiping it away was exhausting, and I was putting it off until I actually showered and went to bed. The martini Cory made me though was doing its job, and I was finally beginning to unwind and relax enough to think straight again.

"I wish Harper would hurry up." Ursula turned to stare out the window where Sheriff Hottie leaned against my railing. He was writing furiously in his small notebook, his cell phone lying on the wooden rail. The background checks had come back on the contestants and their guests. Hopefully, there would be something there, a beacon to guide us in the right direction. So far, we were fumbling without a clue.

"At least the girls learned the second number. Now, all we have to do is add Shae and Janet into it, if they... you know..." Cory trailed off and turned sharply towards the bar. He had a full drink.

"Joey said the doctor released them. They're gonna be tired at tomorrow's rehearsal, but they both plan on being there." Ursula boomed, which made poor Cory drop the jigger onto the bar. "Drag queens don't give up, hon. We're made of stern stock."

"I know, but... Would you come back after someone tried to kill you? I think I would pack my bags and go home." Cory picked up the shaker and poured some bourbon into it. Harper must be about to come in. Maybe now Cory would sit the fuck down.

"I'd come back. Momma wouldn't let some asshole dim her shine. And I'd come back with a passion. I bet those girls do too. Dragons are made with a spine of steel." Urs was getting tipsy. Her face was even flushing a little in a very becoming way. Even without makeup, Ursula was gorgeous. Damn her.

The door opened, and Harper stepped inside. The look he gave me told me all I needed to know.

"Background checks turned up a lot of debt, a DUI, and some parking tickets. I did, however, find out that one of our girls has a degree in agriculture. That would mean he would know about copper sulfate." Harper shrugged and took the drink Cory held out for him.

"So would the internet. I googled poison in the water, and it came up easily. Does anyone in town sell it?" I asked, hoping that might give us a lead.

"Yes, and we already checked. They hadn't sold any in over a month. It was one of the first things the team did when we found out what it was." Harper frowned.

"I figured. You are incredibly hot at your job... I mean very great at your job." I teased and blew him a kiss.

"Looking at Vickie's face in Victor's clothes and hair is really turning me on." He leaned in and gave me a kiss that was polite for company. I wanted more. I always wanted as much of Harper as I could get. However, tonight I was too exhausted to even think about it.

"Nice. I'll be sure to wear the face to bed and smear the makeup all over your pillow." I droned, downing the rest of my drink dand breathing hard. "So, which girl is a farmer?"

"The method actor." He raised his eyebrows. I

mean, the mere thought of Janet as a farmer was comical.

"Benjamin Bradford the Third from Barstow is a method acting farmgirl?" I cackled and held my glass up in the air for Cory to refresh. He rolled his eyes and took it out of my hand. I heard the clink of ice into the shaker and grinned. "Thank you, boo-boo."

"You are so lucky I can't live without you." He said as dramatically as possible.

"Cory's a method actor, too." I chuckled.

"Karen's a farm girl?" Ursula shrugged. "It actually makes sense. Have you seen his lack of a manicure?"

"I don't know about you, but I feel like I've run a marathon today. I am bushed." Harper sipped his drink and gently jostled the amber liquid in his glass as he stared at it. "The water had a blueish tint, and I can't believe they didn't notice that. I mean, would you drink light blue water?"

"I don't think I would have noticed it, probably. Depends on how much I was paying attention. These girls have a lot on their mind," Ursula replied, pinching her face up in deep thought. "The glasses were clear, though."

"I'm just wondering if Lil' Debbie's murder had anything to do with the poison. At first glance, you would think so, but what if it's not? What if the poison was trying to take girls out of the competition, but the murder was something else?" I shivered. My dragtuition was trying to tell me something, but I couldn't quite place my press-ons to it.

"Here you go, sis." Cory handed me my refreshed martini.

"Thanks, love. Cory, have you seen any of the drag sponsors come in for their individual talent rehearsals?"

Cory nodded vigorously. "Oh yeah. That Domino was throwing a fit over Pussina's talent. He really wants those fire effects. Carson was also an asshole. He screamed at Pam multiple times. But the others have been fine. They just sit there and watch and every now and then whisper to their queen."

I turned to Harper, and he was shaking his head with a stupid grin on his face. "Yes, they're coming in tomorrow, and we will be talking to the other sponsors and dancers, too. I sent you an email."

"I haven't checked my email..." I grinned. "Harper Wolfe... I fucking adore you."

"The feeling's mutual."

"Holy fucking shit!" Ursula screamed, jumping to her feet and running up the first few stairs before stopping and turning around to run back down them. Her hand clutching her phone so tightly I thought she might break it.

"Madonna died?" Cory looked terrified.

"No. A text... Judy was getting in her bed and pulled the covers back to find a rattlesnake under there." She looked like she was about to explode.

"You're shitting me!" Harper bellowed. "This case is... Jesus! Let me call the station. Is she still in the room?"

"Girl... I mean handsome... She is *not* in the room. Nor should she *be* in the room. She is standing outside freaking the fuck out." Ursula pursed her lips. "Honey, give me five. I cannot go save Ms. Judy in my house robe."

"Jensen! Great, I thought you were on duty. I need you to go to... Shit, which hotel is she at?" He stared at me, and I shrugged. I had no fucking clue. I glanced over at Cory, who looked deep in thought.

"She's at the Maple Bay. I remember." He said seriously. "She wasn't staying at the same hotel as Lil' Debbie."

"Go to The Maple Bay and call animal control. We seem to have a rattlesnake in one of the rooms, and it didn't get there on its own. You should call Carpenter in and have him dust for prints. I'll be there in about ten minutes." He listened and looked annoyed. Harper was usually patient, but he looked like he was about to explode with frustration. "Do you know which room?"

"Oh, that's easy. It will be the one with the drag queen freaking out in front of it." Cory laughed. "Sorry... It's not funny."

"Ready!" Ursula grabbed her purse and stood by the front door in a red leather jacket and pants.

"How did you do that so fast?" I barked, amazed and astonished at her drag transformation.

"Trust, sis. I could pull on a full face and bodysuit faster than a freshman virgin before he…"

"Yeah, we're on our way." Harper stood and sat down his half-full glass. "Is that really what you're wearing?"

"Oh shit!" I jumped up and ran upstairs. I could not seriously pull off Vicki in the light right now. I threw on her wig and wrapped a scarf around my head, thankful I had been lazy with taking off her makeup. I grabbed one of the long jackets Vicki enjoyed in the chilly months and threw it on with a pair of chunky heels. This would have to do.

A fucking snake…

That was definitely an attempt on her life. Someone was trying to kill my girls.

Chapter Seven

$\mathcal{H}$arper drove like a bat out of hell. His jeep flying down the road with the lights flashing and sirens blaring. I sat in the front seat, and Cory and Ursula sat in the back. It was hard to hear what they were talking about, but it sounded like Cory was asking her questions about the reality show. Once a fan, always a fan.

It didn't take long at all until we pulled into town, and Harper parked in the small parking lot of The Maple Bay Hotel. Jensen and Carpenter were already there talking to a very flustered Judy Ghouland. Her arms were moving around in a rapid motion, and she was almost fluttering with nervous energy. I'd be freaking the hell out too. A mother fucking snake was in her bed.

We pulled up, and as soon as Judy saw Ursula, she ran into her arms. Ursula cooed to her, doing her best to calm her down. Ursula and Judy worked at the same club in Los Angeles, and they were tight. Her cheeks were wet, and her eyes darted everywhere.

"This is why I don't go hiking!" Judy started sobbing. "Someone was trying to kill me, Urs! A snake in my bed."

"Girl, there's been plenty of snakes in your bed," Ursula tried humor, and Judy did chuckle half-heartedly through her tears.

"Yeah, but only their souls were poisonous. Not their bite."

"Jensen? When's animal control getting here?" Harper asked, his voice tired and rugged.

"Should be any moment. Old man Johnson was getting out of bed and said he was on his way."

"How the hell does someone get a rattlesnake? I mean, it's not like you can buy one, is it?" Carpenter gasped. Apparently, he wasn't a fan of snakes. "You don't expect me to try to get prints off that damn thing, do you?"

"Only if it has to be killed. If there are prints on the snake, the perp had to leave them someplace else."

"I don't think you'll find any. We didn't at the murder scene. Chances are if the person was smart enough to wear gloves once..." I shook my head, trying to find a connection. The pageant was the only thing there was. Who wanted the title bad enough to kill? I couldn't imagine any of these girls as killers, especially not after interviewing them.

"I know. But we still have to try. You doing ok, Vicki? It's a good thing we were still going over the interviews." Harper made sure his voice was loud enough for the other officers to hear. They knew he was dating Victor, but if we weren't careful, they might figure out my secret identity.

"Is he keeping you out too late, Ms. Dean? Oh, here comes old man Johnson, now. Shit. He looks annoyed." Jensen laughed.

"He looks drunk." Carpenter slapped Jensen on the arm.

"I'm not going back in there, Urs! I just want to grab my stuff and go home." Judy was hysterical. I mean, her character was a zombified Judy Garland, so it made sense.

"Pull it together, sis. These bitches are trying to scare you." Ursula grabbed her by the upper arms and practically shook her. I think Ursula was starting to lose it, too. I didn't blame her. This whole thing was like a horror show.

I walked over and placed my arm around poor Judy. Ursula looked at me wild-eyed.

"I hate snakes," Ursula admitted as if that explained everything.

"Judy? Do you have any idea who might have done this? Did something happen today with one of the girls or anyone else?" I asked slowly, hoping it might make her focus. Her breath told me that she had been imbibing a little too. Smelled like vodka—my kind of girl.

"No, Ms. Dean. I get along with everyone, even Karen. I don't know why anyone would do this to me. I feel like... like this was a warning or something. What if I keep competing, and the next time it's not a snake but a knife... or a gun? I am... this shit is too cray-cray, and no fucking tiara is worth this." She wiped her eyes and stamped her foot. Lord, she was young and shouldn't have to be going through any of this. None of the girls should be.

"You are one of the favorites to win, Judy. That's why. I know it deep down." Ursula turned and stared at me with her eyes wide. "Vic...ki... I think this has to do with the pageant. It has to."

She was right. This was the third attempt and possible fourth victim to a killer we knew nothing about. Even if Lil' Debbie's killer was a different person, these last two attempts were all about the title of Ms. Cali West Coast. It had to be, or there was no pattern.

One of the first things I learned reading mysteries was there was always a pattern. I interwove those patterns into my plot carefully, letting them unwind and be seen at just the right times. The pattern was everything, and it had to be here. It may be hidden, but with the right questions, anything could be discovered.

"SON OF A BITCH!"

We all turned to the sound of the voice, and I realized it was coming from the open door of Judy's room.

"AHA! GOTCHA!" Old man Johnson's voice boomed from the brightly lit doorway.

I glanced over at Harper, and he looked like he wanted to get in his car and drive away. My man must not be a very big fan of snakes either. There was something about snakes I both admired and feared. The way they could hide was astounding and admirable. It was also why they scared the shit out of me.

Old man Johnson, and I have no idea why they called him that, was not really that old. He was possibly late forties or early fifties, but so incredibly thin that he looked like he had been pulled in a taffy machine. He strode out of the hotel room, holding a bag with the wiggling would-be assassin inside.

Harper actually took a step back. It was cute and made him even more adorable to me. It was healthy to have fears, and Harper was so alpha, so manly, that I had never really seen this side of him before.

"You're not scared of a little snake, are you sheriff?"

"Johnson, if you bring that any closer to me, I'm gonna shoot you. It too." Harper warned.

Jensen clapped him on the back and laughed. Carpenter grabbed his bag and started to head inside the room. He stopped and slowly turned around.

"You don't think there's any more of them inside, do you?" he asked meekly.

"No. I had to search to find this one. He was in the

corner of the closet. No worries, Jensen. It's snake free!" Johnson laughed as he walked over to his truck and sat the bag inside a metal box in the back of his truck. "What do you want me to do with this sheriff?"

"I... uh... release it in Arizona," Harper muttered, a feeble smile crossing his handsome face.

"Release it?"

"Do you think there's any reason to keep it?" Jensen gasped.

"Well, there's a fair black-market trade for snakes that have been turned into venomoids. Seems to me, either someone was a damn good snake handler, or this snake isn't all that dangerous. Would have to test it to make sure." Johnson leaned against his truck and crossed his arms.

"What the hell does that mean?" Harper barked. His patience was thin, even if his biceps were thick. Sorry, I couldn't help myself.

"Well, a venomoid snake has had surgery to remove its venom glands. It could still bite, but it wouldn't be poisonous, just painful. There are lots of idiots out there who think owning a rattlesnake is cool, trust me. They even sometimes remove the fangs, but this one has them intact. It's cruel and disgusting, and those that do it should be locked up for animal cruelty." Johnson spat and pulled out a pack of cigarettes. I used to smoke back when I was a young draglet. I was stressed out enough, right now, to wish I still did.

"How can you tell?" Harper asked curiously.

"Well, there could be scars from the surgery. If not, we would have to see if we could milk it to extract anything and test it. It would be a fairly quick test. I could have Madison do it in the morning." Johnson lit it up and inhaled. Yeah... It smelled better than I wanted it to.

"I didn't even know that was a thing. Can you do that and let us know, please? It would be the difference between attempted murder or a scare tactic." Harper sighed. "This case is getting weirder and weirder with every fucking hour."

"I cannot go back in there, Ursula," Judy said so suddenly and vehemently we all jumped.

"I'll spend the night with you, hon. I can wear this tomorrow. Cory, honey? Would you mind picking me up in the morning so I could make myself decent for human eyes?" Ursula asked sweetly, knowing Cory would walk over hot coals for her.

"Duh!" He grinned.

"You can't stay in that room tonight anyway. We'll be here for a few hours. Let me go talk to the manager. He's been gawking out the damn window the whole time." Harper turned to walk away and quickly turned back to old man Johnson. "And you let me know first thing tomorrow, Johnson. Thank you."

"Do you have everything you need out of your room? I can't really let you take much since we need to dust and infrared everything." Jensen walked over to

Judy and looked like he wanted to give her a hug. Of course, Judy looked a lot more like Joe right now.

"I have everything I really need. It's fine. Can I come back in the morning?" Judy asked sweetly, trying her best to flirt with the exceptionally handsome officer. All of the deputies in Maple Bay were hired for their insta-hottie looks, or you would assume. It was rather alarming.

"We will be done by then, and if we have to take anything, I will leave you a list on the desk, okay?" Jensen really was a sweetie. I had grown fond of the young man ever since he helped me out during my own harrowing experience with murder.

"Come on, Judy. Vicki, honey. Are you going back to Victor's place?" Ursula asked. I nodded, and she grinned at me. "Please tell Vic I will see him tomorrow at the rehearsal."

It was a long night for us. I stayed outside for a bit, thinking over everything I still didn't know with Cory. Harper and his boys were still checking the room for any evidence. It was longer than I wished it would have been. Should have made Cory drive separately. When he emerged, I knew they found nothing helpful inside.

But if that snake came back venomous, it was only a matter of time until someone else died.

If it wasn't... We could be dealing with multiple individuals who may or may not be connected.

I wasn't going to sleep much tonight.

Chapter Eight

"That was a total shit show." I wiped my face with my makeup remover sheet. I hadn't had the time to do my normal heavier underpainting, so it was coming off much faster than usual.

"Why did it have to be a snake?" Harper groaned, sitting down in the corner chair and removing his shoes.

"I still think you're the butchest of all, honey." I teased, pursing my lips and winking at him in the mirror. He responded by tossing a rolled-up sock at my back.

"Did anyone ever tell you you're hilarious?" He wasn't very good at being sarcastic. It always sounded too sincere.

"Did anyone tell you that I love you, Sheriff Hottie?" I turned around on the vanity stool and stared at him. He was gorgeous, and I still couldn't believe that a man like this could ever love me. He was ripped right out of the romance novels and put on this Earth for people to fantasize over. Except, he wasn't a fantasy for me.

I pinched myself. Yeah... Reality.

"Once or twice," He stood up and unbuttoned his khaki shirt, unfastening the badge. He fumbled with the clasp. He had large fingers and always struggled with undoing the heavy metal. It was cute and normalizing. So was his fear of snakes.

"Ah..." He pulled his finger back quickly and stuck it in his mouth. "Fucking pin." He laid it down on the small table by the chair.

"Can't you order those badges I always see on TV that's like a magnet or something? I hate watching you stick yourself every night." I wiped away the last of the makeup and stared at him in the mirror's reflection.

"Well, that would stop me from pricking myself every night, wouldn't it?" He stuck his tongue out at me. "And you always make me feel so much better after I get an ouchie."

"Ah... Does my big bad sheriff need someone to make him feel better?" I stood up and walked over to him, slowly lowering myself down until I was sitting in his lap. What I really wanted to do was to straddle him, but momma was way too tired for that, both mentally and physically.

He nuzzled his nose against my neck, and I leaned against his hard bare chest.

"I am at a loss." He kissed the soft flesh of my cheek.

"Yeah... I think... If that snake was venomous..."

"God, can we not talk about snakes, please?" He groaned.

"If it's venomous, then this might be all by one person. The why is still questionable. The title, or revenge? It has to be one of the two." I pressed myself harder into him and his arms wrapped around me, holding me tightly.

"If it's not venomous, then we may be dealing with multiple suspects? That's what I was wondering too. Someone was taking advantage of the situation... But if that's the case, they had been planning this all along. Buying a... whatever it was he called it, on the black market would not be a fast purchase." He shivered. "God, imagine driving with that in the car..." He shivered.

"Why do you hate snakes so much? I mean, I'm not a fan either, but this fear of yours seems a little unhealthier." I chuckled, my breath making his neck get goose pimples.

He sighed, and I scooted down, placing my head on his thick shoulder. I could feel his steady inhale and exhale in my hair. It was so calming.

"My brother had a pet boa constrictor when he was in high school. He's... well, you know, a few years older than me, and he used to tease me about letting it loose in my room so it could eat me. I had the worst dreams about it and barricaded my door every night after checking to make sure the snake was still in its enclosure. Shit... The nightmares that snake caused me were... I guess I've never gotten over it. I've been terrified of snakes ever since."

"That's it?" I looked up at him and grinned, trying to not laugh at his childhood trauma. "I guess I expected something... scarier."

"Hey, I was like ten or eleven when he started doing that. He told me that he didn't need to open the door to get the snake inside. He could slip him in through the vents, which, I mean, I know now that he couldn't have done that. It was a big snake, and the vent was screwed into the wall."

"Oh, I think you would be surprised what small holes a snake can get through."

"I know that my snake can get into..."

I bolted upright. "How did that snake get into the hotel room and placed under the covers? Judy's door was locked. Someone had to have a key or have gotten one from a housekeeper or something, right?"

"I forgot to tell you. Her window hadn't been locked. I was really hoping when I found the window unlocked we might pull a print." He grimaced. "All we found were some fibers, and yes, they are being analyzed. Hopefully, we will get some information tomorrow. Jensen was driving them up tonight."

"I like Jensen." I kissed the side of his lips.

"Hopefully, you don't like him more than you like me?" He kissed me back.

We did finally go to sleep, and we were both totally exhausted.

Chapter Nine

The next day Harper and I dragged ourselves out of bed and stumbled to the shower. I had to make an appearance at the club this morning while the girls were going through the third-night opening number and reviewing the two they already learned. Somehow, Roy was going to have to integrate Shae and Janet into what the rest of the girls learned yesterday. I knew he had a plan to keep their movements simple, but it was still going to be a lot for them to learn all at once.

The show must go on.

We barely spoke as we got dressed. I knew this week was going to be tiring, but this was on a whole different level. Momma needed her eight hours, or she started to look like Hagatha in drag, and I couldn't have that. Raven was known for being gorgeous. Vicki was pretty in a completely different way. She was more soccer mom with class.

I packed Vicki's bag and carried it downstairs, and placed it by her wig.

"Should we make coffee or just go into town and grab some?" Harper stretched his arms above his head. "This is my last clean uniform. I have to do some laundry tonight, or the sheriff is gonna smell bad."

"I like the way the sheriff smells." I walked into the kitchen and pulled out my coffee pods. "I can't drive to get coffee unless I have some coffee first."

"Then you better make an espresso, too. We can add it. I think I need it, you vixen." He chuckled.

"Don't blame me if you can't keep your hands off the goods, Harper." I pressed the pod in and remembered to grab a travel mug and put it in place before I hit brew. Yes, I was that tired.

"We're meeting Domino... Can you believe that's his name? He sounds like some two-bit mafioso. Anyway, we're meeting him at two at the station. I wanted to keep him away from the girls. Then we have a few more interviews with the other producers."

"Sponsors, honey. They're called drag sponsors."

"I really hope I never hear the word sponsor or pageant ever again when this is over." He mumbled.

"Me too. Aren't you glad I'm not one of those girls who want a tiara and a sash? Though I do think a title would look great on me." I teased. It was half-assed because I was fighting to keep my eyes open and stifling the yawn that continuously threatened to erupt at any moment.

"You have a title." He walked in and wrapped his arms around me. "Bestselling novelist and boyfriend to the sheriff. Do you want me to buy you a sash to wear?" He kissed me on the top of the head. "Oh, thank God. Can I have this one?"

"Why should you go first." I pouted.

"It's better to caffeinate the guy with the gun." He said seriously.

"Good point. Let me brew the espresso so I can pour it in." I grabbed a new pod and popped the old one out.

Harper reached around me and grabbed the mug before going over to the table and sitting down.

He enjoyed his coffee while I waited for the espresso and then my own cup to brew. I split the shot between us and stirred it in before grabbing my bags. Harper strapped on his belt with all of his sheriffy things attached to it, and we walked to our cars.

"Let me know what you find out. Just text me." I said before kissing him and walking around his truck to my car.

"Fine, but I'd rather hear your voice." He pouted, and I had to stop myself from going to kiss him again.

"If I can call, I will when I get your text, Mr. Co-dependent."

"As long as it's with you, I don't think I mind that

title!" He shouted before getting in his truck and pulling slowly out of my driveway.

I followed behind him until he headed to the station, and I made my way over to Rumors. I was on time, but I knew Ursula was going to be late. She texted me that Cory was picking her up when I was making coffee. He would let her into my house so she could get ready and then bring her back. That meant I was on my own with the queens and a possible psychopath.

Great. Must be a Wednesday.

"Hey, diva!" Henry called as I walked through the door. "The excitement of this pageant is killing me."

"Don't tease," I snipped, pointing my finger at him and wagging it furiously.

"I know, sorry. Too soon, right?" He grabbed some stuff and started walking to the patio. "You holding up, ok, Vic?"

"I'll let you know when it's over."

Henry disappeared behind the drapes. "You have a horde of homo's with heels out here."

I threw down my murse and walked to the main door, unlocking it and looking at the girls all huddled together. They were looking around in different directions. Yeah, they were freaking out.

"Victor! Are you ok? We were worried that something had happened to you too," Vivienne whispered, which was actually a yell. She only understood a stage whisper, apparently.

"I'm fine. I just had an appointment I couldn't miss, and sadly, I have to run point with the pageant and the police. That's why Ursula came in to help me. I heard the number looked great. Shae... Janet... I am so happy to see you two." I touched each of them on the arm as they walked by. I wanted them to know that I was on their side. That way, maybe one of them would share something in confidence they didn't share with Vicki or the sheriff. I didn't have much hope for it to work, but I was giving it the old queenly try.

"Yesterday sucked. If I ever throw up that much ever again, someone please bash me in the head with a shoe," Dammit Janet quipped and then threw her hand over her mouth in shock. "I didn't mean that."

"They know, honey. We can say whatever we want today after surviving almost being murdered." Shae looked the other girls in the eyes, daring them to say anything. They just agreed with a head nod.

"I'm just glad you're back. I don't want to win this bitch because I'm the last girl standing. I want to kick your asses when you're all at your best." Eatta Twinkie said wryly.

"Who's to say who'll be standing," Judy looked like she had barely slept last night.

"Tell me more about that. I can't believe there was a snake in your bed. Someone really is trying to do us all in, aren't they?" Pam From Payroll grabbed Judy by the arm and led her over towards the stage. "I'm sorry, hon. I would have shit myself."

"Mmm... Do us in? God... I hate that phrase. Can't we just admit that someone is a killer? Maybe one of us, maybe not... But there's still a murderer in our midst." Pussina threw her bag down and looked at it. She picked it back up and zipped it tightly. "Mmm... Just in case."

"Girls, Roy will be here in a few to review the numbers with you. He'll add Janet and Shae into the second number. Stretch and get ready, so we're not wasting time," I said sadly, knowing that their experience here was forever tarnished.

"You can gossip, bitches, but stretch while you do it!" Vivienne said in a pretty dead-on Bette Davis impression. She was fantastic at impressions and was planning on doing them for her talent.

Every one of the queens pulled out a water bottle from their murses and waved them up in the air in solidarity. It made them giggle, which was nice to hear. This whole thing had been way too serious.

"Ladies!" Roy walked in and clapped his hands. "Good, we're stretching, and Shae and Janet are back, I see. Ladies, if you two will sit and watch, I'll have the other girls do it so you can judge them. Be cruel." He sat his bag down at the foot of the stage and waved at me. "Where's Cory and Ursula?"

"They're ok," I assured everyone. "Just running a little late."

"So tell me about this snake, Judy," Valerie asked as she bent down and touched her toes. She was wearing a stripper heel so steep I wasn't sure how she walked in them. That took talent.

The girls gossiped about Judy's tale of escaping death and the cute officers that they had seen around or she spoke to. Eatta pointed to me, and everyone nodded.

"What?" I rolled my eyes.

"Your boyfriend is like extra, sis. That man is so fine, I'd drink his sweat." Eatta cackled, and the rest of the girl's air clapped in a circle.

"I don't call him Sheriff Hottie for nothing, girls." I blushed. I was proud to be Harper's boyfriend, and it made me feel good to have the girls jealous of my beau-hunk.

"Alright. I don't see enough stretching, ladies," Roy clapped and winked at me.

"I bet that man is packing." Valerie elbowed Vivienne in the side. She looked over at her and frowned.

"Your elbow is so bony, I thought it was a knife. Eat." Vivienne retorted and picked up her heels. "Heels on ladies before Roy starts throwing more side-eye at us."

Chapter Ten

The girls were doing fine, and Shae and Janet had come back with a mission. They were on fire during rehearsal and picked up the choreography faster than expected. When I left, they were learning the third routine, and Cory had found time for them to rehearse their talent part of the competition.

I said my goodbyes and drove over to my small cottage, which Vickie Dean LLC owned. I parked as close to the front door as I could. It was usually safe from prying eyes, but I grabbed my bags and hurried inside. I loved my actual house, I did, but my heart wanted to call this place home. One day I would build a house here on the land I owned and keep this small retreat as my office.

But that day was not now. I still held tightly onto my secret of being mystery writer and bestselling author Vicki Dean. Only my publisher, editor, boyfriend, the bestie with the chestie, and now Ursula knew the truth of her identity. It felt good to share that with my new friend. I was glad that we had become as close as we had. I had missed that kind of sisterhood.

I walked into my small back room that served as a storage place—a day bed set against the wall for those times when I really needed to take a nap. But today, I was back here to sit at the small vanity so I could beat my face – hard. I had enough time today to make sure Vicki was as perfect as she could get.

I grabbed my dark brown and clown white and began her underpainting. There was something therapeutic about putting on makeup. The feel of the sponges and brushes were like tiny caresses as they tickled my skin, changing the shape of my face's structure. Victor's nose disappeared, and Vicki's took its place. Her cheekbones covered my own, and the dark bags I was sporting melted away under the power of drag.

I grabbed my base and highlighter and covered the kabuki theatre on my face with a nice neutral skin tone that matched the rest of me—my highlighter working with the underpaint to emphasize the changes between myself and my creation.

I powdered lightly and started working on the smoky eye that Vicki preferred. It was subtle but dramatic in its own way. Vicki didn't wear a lot of eyeliner. Just a small emphasis on the bottom and top was all she needed. Her rouge and lipstick came next, and I finished her with a light setting powder to keep her firmly in place.

Even without the wig, I no longer saw myself. I sat up straight and assumed Vicki's posture and mannerisms. They had become second nature to me, now.

I gently placed her locks on my head and pulled my own hair through the front lace, and blended it perfectly into the human hair on the wig. I paid a ton of money for these wigs, dyed to perfectly match my own hair so there would never be a wig line for someone to clock. I sprayed it lightly and slid on the small pads that created her figure. Slim, yet soft and subtle. Vicki's hourglass appeared as I pulled on one of her outfits. The skirt and shirt followed by the jacket that accentuated her bosom.

I loved this moment. A new person stood in front of me, looking back through the mirror. I was giving author realness with a bit of flair, and I winked at myself. Looking fine, Vicki Dean.

It was showtime.

I locked my door and then drove over to the Sheriff's Station. I parked in the back and walked around to enter the front door. I shouldn't have done that. Betty Davis was standing outside as if she knew I was coming.

"So it's true. You're helping the department again?" Betty eyed me as if she already knew the answer. Gossip travels fast in a small town.

"It is. The case is quite a mystery, and I've been asked to be a part of the investigation as a civilian consultant. The boys and I enjoy working together, and it's great research to watch them in action." I started to walk around her, and she shifted back in front of me.

"Betty... You know I can't comment on anything." I said with as much spice as I could muster.

"Oh, come on, Vicki. So far, I've heard about the murder, and that is... I mean, a drag queen who was impaled in the head by a stiletto is newsworthy." She crossed her arms and grinned widely. She loved to gossip, and any opportunity to break a story on the local radio station made her positively gleeful.

"I'm not going to comment on that." I sighed. Dealing with Betty was always confrontational. She was a powerful woman, and I admired her a lot. But she was also annoying and would do anything for a lead to share with her listeners.

"That means it's true." She cocked her head and waited.

"It means I'm not commenting," I smirked, which made the smile melt off her face.

"You are such a stick in the mud, do you know that? I thought us ladies were supposed to support one another." She countered.

"It's an ongoing investigation. You want information, you should talk to the department."

"Sheriff Wolfe is tight-lipped about any of this. Believe me, I've tried. What about the two drag queens who were taken to the hospital? Any comments on that?" She rolled her eyes.

"Actually, yes. They have made a full recovery and are back rehearsing for the pageant. My assistant Cory is helping his friend, Victor, as you well know, and he texted me this morning that they were back in the competition. It's wonderful news, and that's what you should report. I'll be there, I'm sure. I love a good drag queen." Shit. As soon as the words tumbled from my lips, I knew I had made a mistake. Betty would tell all of Maple Bay that I would be in attendance at the pageant because I was a big fan of drag queens. She loved any opportunity to report on Maple Bay's most famous citizen now that she was no longer a recluse. Seriously, she even started a Vicki Dean watch for a while that talked about me visiting businesses in town. It was very annoying.

"Well, I know the town is excited about the pageant, and they'll be thrilled that you are too. See you around, Vicki." She turned and sashayed away. She was such a pain in my ass.

I stood there frozen in place. What the fuck had I just done? Why did I have to open my mouth? Vicki Dean can't be at the pageant because Raven was going to be there, and I couldn't wear two drag personas at the same time. I had to emcee the damn thing. How was Vicki going to explain not showing up because, with Betty Davis, I would have to? The town would be disappointed if I didn't make an appearance now. Shit.

I forced these spinning thoughts out of my mind as quickly as I could. My sexy sheriff was waiting inside for me to begin the interviews with the contestant's guests. There were a couple of them that I really wanted to talk to. Someone had to know something. They all couldn't be excellent liars, could they? We needed a break, and we needed it badly before someone else got hurt, or worse, killed.

I opened the doors and walked in. The lone female officer, Letitia, was sitting at the front desk, looking bored. She was fairly new. Harper hired her a couple months ago, and she had only met Vicki once. She knew Victor incredibly well, though. Harper really liked her and for her to be on desk duty meant that Andrew, the usual guy was out today.

"Hi, Vicki. Sheriff Wolfe said to send you back to his office when you arrived." She waved as the phone rang. "Maple Bay Sheriff Station, is this an emergency? Lord... No, Adina, we cannot come out because kids are playing soccer in the street. You live in a cul de sac."

I chuckled as I walked through the office, waving to Jensen and Carpenter before stopping in front of Harper's closed door. Harper was on the phone and waved for me to come in. I closed the door behind me and sat down in the stiff metal chair that was hell on my back. I told him I was going to give his office a makeover. I don't think he was a big fan of that idea. He liked things the way they are.

"Great. Thank you, that helps us quite a bit. You too." He hung up the phone.

"What was that?" I crossed my ankles and blew him a quick kiss.

"That was the analysis on the fibers. I'm surprised you didn't call and cuss me out."

I looked at him as if he had three heads. Why would he say that?

"I forgot to text you this morning." He grinned, knowing I had to be way too tired to have forgotten.

"You bastard," I said lazily. "Honestly, I got so caught up with making sure the wheels were staying on the road for the pageant, I forgot, too. So…"

"Non-venomous. A Veno…" He puffed his cheeks out in frustration. Too cute…

"Venomoid, honey," I smirked. "So that snake wasn't meant to kill Judy, just scare her to death."

"I hate that phrase. Has anyone ever truly died from fright?" He leaned his chin on his hand and propped his elbow on his desk, letting the weight of it rest there.

"Yes. Many… many times. It's well documented." I opened my eyes wide. "I'm still so tired I can barely think."

"Yeah. We have to go to bed at a decent hour tonight." Harper said seriously. "I think I could sleep for an entire day when all of this is over."

"I suppose they might not have known the snake was no longer venomous. But they did feel safe enough to put it in the bed and cover it up. To do that, I think I would have to know it couldn't bite and kill me." My mind was working through the possibilities at a pace it could barely keep up with. I needed… "Coffee. Can someone please bring me a large cup of coffee?"

Harper stood and opened his door. "Jensen? What are you doing?"

"I'm… I'm adding the new files to the computer. Why?"

"Can you or someone else go and get two coffees next door, please? Maybe add a shot of espresso? I think Vicki and I both need it after last night."

"So, does that mean there are two different people committing the crimes or are they still connected? Maybe getting rid of Lil' Debbie was personal in some way but the others… The killer just wants them out of the pageant?"

"Maybe? Maybe not? The fibers that we recovered from the window were from a pair of thick cotton work gloves. The tan kind you would find on construction sites. Those fibers were not found in the hotel. But we did get a hit on the partial, well, what we thought was a dirt print found in the doorway of the room." Harper walked over and stood behind me. His breathing soft and controlled. My heart sped up. It always did when he was this close.

"I don't remember you mentioning a print…"

"I think I mentioned it. Shit, I don't know anymore. It wasn't much, so I didn't think it would result in anything. I figured it might have been Lil' Debbie's or one of the dancers. The state sent it back, and from the width of the print, which was mainly at the front of the shoe, it would probably be from a size 11-12 Nike tennis shoe, they believe." Harper said from behind me, his hands resting on the back of my chair. I knew he wanted to touch me as badly as I wanted him to.

"Anything else you held back from me?"

"Don't be like that. You weren't really involved when we... No, that's it." He chuckled. "You sit so straight when you get angry, and I'm sure I told you."

"Hmm... Maybe you did. I was really tired. The dancers are coming in today. Let's be sure to ask for shoe sizes or at least glance down. Who's first?"

Harper walked around and sat on the edge of his desk. His knees just a foot from my own and grinned.

"I think it's one of the dancers. They really want to leave since they are no longer performing." Harper sighed.

I wanted to leave too. A Caribbean vacation sounded fantastic right now.

"Well, we can't all have what we want, I guess." I huffed. I needed that coffee, now, or I was about to get really real up in here with these assholes.

I was on edge, and that was never a good thing. I had to remember that Vicki was a woman – not a drag queen. Even if she really was. I buried my drag genetics as deeply as I could. If they erupted, there would be no hiding the fact that Vicki was a glamazon.

I didn't wait for much longer. Carpenter knocked on the door and delivered my caffeine. I breathed a sigh of relief as I took a sip. Even the smell unknotted my shoulders and soothed me. I took a tentative sip. You know that moment when you see if it's so hot you scald your lips. It was pretty damn hot, but not so bad I had to blow into it.

"You ready, babe?" Harper breathed heavily. This was weighing heavy on him - his job always did. But being a sheriff in a small town wasn't supposed to be this insane. First, it was the mayor's murder, and now, not even half a year later, a dead drag queen with a pump impaled into her skull. This town would need some serious PR.

"As I'll ever be, I guess." I stood, and Harper grabbed hold of my arm and guided me into the small conference room. We took a seat on the far side of the table, and I prepared myself for what was about to happen. Would we find out anything that would help us? I doubted it but wanted to have hope... I was just running low.

If we didn't find out something that could lead us to the next clue. We may never.

Chapter Eleven

"*L*eticia, you can send the first person in?" Harper said after calling her on the intercom.

Jensen brought in a young Latino with a face that looked like Botticelli created it and a body from Crunch Gym. He had to be someone's dancer. "Hi. I'm Gio Garcia. Should I sit here?"

"Sure, Gio. Thanks for coming. This is Vicki Dean. She's helping the department with the investigation."

"Hi." He nodded. He had no idea who I was, bless him. He looked like a boy who watched The housewives instead of reading. When you had a face and body like that... Well, reading wasn't something you did at night.

"Can you tell us a little about your relationship with Barry?" Harper asked, and Gio looked at him strangely.

"Lil' Debbie," I added, knowing that was what Gio always called her.

"Yeah, ok. LD and I became friends at the club in Long Beach. Me and some friends liked to go dancing there, and she grabbed me when I was on the dance floor and pulled me over to the bar to talk to me. She liked the way I moved and wondered what it would take for me to dance backup for her. I said cash, of course. I've been dancing with her for two years, almost." He placed his clasped hands on the table.

"I can see why she chose you. Can you think of anyone who might want to hurt Barry... er... Lil' Debbie?" Harper leaned in towards him, turning on his charm. I could get jealous and cut a bitch up in here real quick if I didn't know better.

"I mean... yeah... There were a lot of people who didn't like her. She could be a real piece of work, you know? She had her own way of doing things, and that rubbed some people the wrong way." He shrugged.

"How was your relationship with Lil' Debbie?" I added, smiling as sweetly as I could. Gio was not impressed. He looked over at Harper and answered.

"It was ok. I mean, she was a hard woman. If you messed up one of her routines or didn't have the energy she wanted you to have... She could make you feel like a piece of shit, you know? But we got along ok. We weren't really friends or anything... Few people were friends with her. The other girls at the bar couldn't stand her, but the audience loved her. She could really turn it out, you know? She could have won this bitch and been Ms. California or whatever. Shit! The amount she spent on those gowns alone was... She was really proud of it and planned on surprising everyone. I just can't believe it was for nothing, you know what I'm saying?"

"Can you think of anyone who might have wanted her dead?" Harper said seriously. I had to stop a smirk from spreading across my face because Gio sat back and all of a sudden looked remorseful.

"Dead? I don't think anyone I know could have... I mean, she was a bitch, but she was our bitch. Her ex was a con, though. Of course, I think he's back in jail, so it couldn't have been him." Gio crossed his arms and made sure to flex. He was trying to flirt badly, and Harper was acting like he was into it.

"Yeah? Well, I guess it couldn't have been him. How about anyone else here at the pageant? Would her sponsor be mad that she was planning on leaving Long Beach and moving to San Francisco?"

"What?" Gio gasped. "Is that real? What a fucking... I didn't know that. Heather would have been pissed, but... I mean, she isn't even here. She's back in Long Beach, still. They were friends, though. Like Heather knew LD better than anyone." Gio sighed. "She didn't even tell us, man... Was she going to go with that asshole Domino? Do you know? Have you met him? He's like the nelliest of the nells, man. His wrists are so limp he couldn't throw a baseball. Total asshat. Just because he has a fetish... He's a freak."

This was going no place helpful. I glanced down underneath the table, and Gio had small feet, which wasn't a surprise. He was a muscular five-eight at best. That shoe print belonged to a much larger man.

"Gio, hon... I think that's all for today." I quipped, ready to move to the next interview.

"Hey, can Marcus and I go back home? There's really no reason for us to stay around." Gio frowned.

"Sorry, but for now, we're asking everyone to stay in town. I was told that your pass would still be honored by the pageant coordinator even if... Well, you know..." I trailed off, feeling like a class A butthole.

Gio left, and Lil' Debbie's other dancer had no more info than Gio did. She was a hard person to get along with. That seemed to be what everyone who ever met her thought, but that wasn't enough to kill her, was it? He also had a shoe size even smaller than Gio's.

The next person to be interviewed was Carson DeVoor, Pam From Payrolls sponsor. He was led in by Jensen, and he sat down and looked at us gruffly.

"Mr. DeVoor, thank you for meeting with us today," Harper said calmly before picking up his coffee and taking a quick sip. I had downed mine.

"I'm not sure why I'm here." Carson frowned. He had a nasal voice that cut through the room. "It would be nice to know what the hell is going on. My girl is scared out of her mind."

"I'm sure she is. There are four contestants that have been attacked. The pageant has hired a guard to be in attendance at all events, and they are doing everything they can to keep them safe while they're at any sponsored event." I jumped in quickly. Joey had contacted everyone involved and told them what was happening.

"What about when they're in their hotel rooms or walking on the street?" He narrowed his eyes and pointed his finger at Harper. "Shouldn't the force be doing more than they currently are?"

"We're doing everything we can to find the person responsible, Mr. DeVoor." Harper spat back, his face stoic. He was trying hard to rein his emotions in. Blowing up would not help us with the questions we needed him to answer. You got more flies with honey than vinegar.

"You're that writer, huh?" He glanced over at me.

"I am. Mr. DeVoor, did you know Lil' Debbie?" I tried to put us back on track. He was hostile and emotional, and I couldn't blame him. I knew that he had invested a lot of time, money, and energy into Pam From Payroll. All sponsors did, and most of the time, they were usually good friends, too.

"I did. She's been in the Ms. Cali system for a while, so of course, I knew her. She was a hell of a talented performer and could turn a look better than most, even if most of her wardrobe was busted. I think she would have done really well this year if she had been... you know... given the opportunity."

"We've heard that from multiple people. Pam is one of the girls that's expected to be at the top, isn't she?" I smiled as if this was some gossip that I had heard. He nodded and smirked.

"She is. She and Judy have been runner-ups up for the last few years, and one of them will probably win. But we've thought that before. If another girl is better, then the other girl will win. It's frustrating when you walk in as the favorite but are out shown by another competitor. It's just the way it is, I guess." He sat back in his chair, relaxing a little.

"So, the pageant is fair, you think? I mean, the judging, I suppose. Sorry, I'm a little new to all of this." He nodded, seeming to get caught up in my excitement.

"Yes. It is, and I am very proud of that fact. My bar in San Diego was one of the first bars to come on board to this new national competition. I have always been pleased by the way it's been run. Joey and his team do a great job. That is until this year, of course." He frowned and stared me down.

"No one could have known that... You know what it is, I'm trying to say. It's horrible. Do you mind if I call you Carson? You can feel free to call me Vicki." He nodded. "I understand what you feel, Carson. You knew her, but did you know her well or just from the competitions?"

"I knew her. I would be surprised if you found

anyone who knew her very well, though. She could be brash and loud, but in reality, I think she was painfully shy... The real person underneath the act, you know. Barry was a bit of a loner."

"So, you did know him, personally?" He nodded and placed his hands on the table.

"Yeah. Barry was originally from San Diego and got his start at my bar. This was... maybe seven years ago. He moved to Long Beach shortly after, and the next thing I know, he has a new drag name and is doing the pageant circuit. I was surprised by it. Barry wasn't one of those people that I thought would make drag a career. I thought it was just a passing fancy at the time. But he did very well for himself."

I nodded. The background check had shown that he lived in San Diego before Long Beach. But the rest was new information. Queens were usually paid under the table.

"Do you know anyone involved with the pageant..."

"That would commit murder?" He laughed. "We're a bunch of gay guys and drag queens who like to have fun and kiki. This is almost like a club we're in, and even though it's a competition, no one wants to win bad enough to kill someone. That's just crazy. I know these people. No... I can't believe that it's any of these people. I know it's not." He said seriously.

"Do you know anyone that might have wanted to kill Barry?" Harper added. "Someone else that isn't involved with the pageant.

"He has an ex-con boyfriend that's a hot mess. When they broke up, he messed up Barry's face really good. But the last I heard, he was in prison, so... No, I guess I don't. He deserved better than this, though. Barry could be a bitch, but all he ever really wanted was to belong." Carson looked stricken as if he had cared for Barry in his own way.

Harper looked at me, and I nodded. There wasn't anything else that Carson could tell us. He seemed to be sincerely moved at Lil' Debbie's death. He was the first person to know him in a way that none of the others did. Could the murderer be someone from Lil' Debbie's past? Were we looking in the wrong places?

A couple of the other girls had dancers with them, and they knew nothing. They had never spoken to Lil' Debbie and were honestly worried about their own safety. It was the same with the makeup and stylists that accompanied them to the pageant. No one knew anything, but they were all on edge.

Jensen opened the door, and the last of our interviews came in for the day. This was the one I was the most curious about. I didn't know Domino from my time in San Francisco, but that didn't mean I didn't know about him. He was not known for being nice or fair to the girls he took under his wing. He ruled over them with an iron fist and made decisions for some of the girls that led to health problems or worse. He liked to pump his stable of drag queens with silicone and filler. I had been surprised that Pussina looked as natural as she did. If she didn't win this year, her face could look completely different next year. There was a lot about drag I didn't like. That should be a person's own decision, not their bosses.

"Domino... Just Domino." Jensen looked at us and made a confused face behind Domino's back as he walked to the chair and sat down. He had an air of superiority about him that made me want to rub the smug look off his face. Like I said, I knew of him, and I didn't like what I knew.

"Domino? Do you have a last name? All of the paperwork submitted to the pageant only had..." Harper asked before Domino held his hand up suddenly and waved it.

"No... No... Just Domino. I had it legally changed a while ago. I'm like Cher, you see."

Woh! Did this mother fucker just compare himself to our lordess and diva, the one and only, Cher? I had to hold back the shade I needed to throw.

"That's a bold choice," I smirked. "What was your last name before you changed it, please?"

"Danny Rossi. I never felt much like a Danny, you understand." He shrugged. "It didn't have no mystique."

"That accent... You're from New York?" Harper scooted towards the table and placed his hand's palm down upon it.

"The Bronx. Though I haven't lived there in a while. I always felt like I belonged in Frisco, you know."

He had a way of ending sentences with what normally sounded like a question but instead came across like a statement. It was uncomfortable for some reason.

"When did you move to San Francisco? It's lovely, but I've always thought New York was too." I tried to act interested. It was hard work when all I wanted to do was slap the table and make him confess. I just had this feeling about him but was it tinged with my own disgust for him, or was it something more. My instincts were off.

"When I was twenty-two. About ten years or so, you know what I mean." He winked and smiled at me, and I had to move my hands out of my lap to under my legs. I was afraid I might reach across and slap him. I think he just called me old. That is not a way to treat a lady, even if she did have to shave.

"What made you interested in being a sponsor to drag queens, Mr. Domino?" Harper took over and reached down, and patted me on my thigh. He knew I was feeling hot under the Spanx.

"I started as a showrunner in a club in New York at a local drag bar and loved it. When I moved to Frisco, I found some uh... investors," He meant crooks, "to invest in my new bar, and I started my own. We're one of the premier drag bars on the West Coast. I'm proud of it, you know. I had a girl who wanted to do a pageant, so I spotted her the fees and bought her a nice dress." I'm sure it was stolen, "I went to it cause I wanted to support her. She was my girl, you see. I loved it and started looking into it and found out that I was pretty good at guiding and molding these girls like they were clay to be the best they could be at these competitions. I have four state champions under my belt and one national champion. Those are really good stats."

"You are Pussina's sponsor, right? Had you spoken to Lil' Debbie at all before the competition?" I said quickly, hoping to catch him off-guard.

"You've done some research, I see, or someone's been spilling the goods on me." He chuckled. "Yeah, I spoke to her about a month ago. She was thinking of moving, and a friend of mine told me about it, so I reached out. Lil' Debbie was a damn good queen, and under my guidance, I think I could have brought her all the way to the top. She thought about it and decided to stay with her current sponsor. Then she called me and told me she was reconsidering. I offered her a job at the club as a part of my showgirls. I think she was going to say yes, but she wasn't given a chance, you see. She died before she gave me her answer." He took a deep breath and slowly released it as he shook his head. "I can't believe she's dead or that it happened here at the pageant. It's a... horrible. She really wanted out of her situation, and I wanted to help her and help myself, you know. Having her and Pussina on my team would have made those other assholes pissed."

"She was going to tell you here at the pageant?"

Domino nodded. "When was the last time you spoke to her?"

"Let's see... Maybe a week before." He pulled out his cell phone and scrolled down. "Yeah... Actually, six days before her death. Last Tuesday. She's been with Heather, her current sponsor, for a while, but she knew she needed better if she wanted to ever win. Heather's not a shark, you see."

"Did she ever say anything to you about someone who might be out..."

"No... We just talked drag and salary. She wanted new gowns for every pageant and four backup dancers, and a chance to sing live. I told her I'd need to hear her sing before I could commit to that. I've been burned by a sparrow who sounded more like a crow before." He sat back and crossed his leg. He had huge feet. However, he didn't seem to be the type who wore sneakers. These were shiny leather dress shoes with a metal tip. He dressed more like an old school gangster, and I couldn't imagine him in something as pedestrian as sneakers.

"Nice shoes. Do you always wear dress shoes, Domino?"

"Look at me. Dress for success has always been my motto. Suits and shoes at work and a smoking jacket and slippers at home. You like them?" He smiled, and I noticed his gold tooth catch the light.

"They're very nice. Is that sharkskin?"

"Good eye. But you're one of those fancy writer

chicks, so I guess you would know class when you see it." His grin turned my stomach.

"I definitely do," I answered pointedly. I'm sure it went right over his head.

"I think that's all for now. If we have anything else, we will let you know. Thank you for your time, Domino."

"You two coming to the show? Should be exciting."

"We'll see. We do have some work to do." Harper huffed.

"Domino? One last thing. Where were you when Lil' Debbie was murdered?" I asked slowly so his thick head could understand I was looking at him as a suspect.

"Who me? I didn't kill that dame. I was driving back to San Francisco with my assistant because we had a special guest at the bar. I was either on the road or in the city when it happened. Feel free to check my GPS on the car or the footage from my security cams at the bar. You asking this of everyone?" He stared me down.

"Why, of course, we are."

"I see. Have a great day, then." He stood up and walked out. The back of his suit jacket had 'Domino' in purple lettering. Of course, it did.

"What did we learn?" I turned to Harper.

"That we still know nothing." He sighed and grasped my hand in his.

"I feel like it's right in front of us, but we can't see it. I was sure it was…"

"I know. I wondered myself. He does act like a two-bit gangster from one of those old movies, though, accent and all."

"Rehearsals should be over now. Let's go back and see if Cory and Ursula discovered anything."

I really needed a drink, and Ursula and I were supposed to perform at the bar tonight. I needed to change drag and figure out what it was I was gonna do. I also needed to try to talk Ursula into doing a little breaking and entering tonight if she was willing. I knew she would be.

Chapter Twelve

We discussed our day and the nothing that we learned from it over a quick cocktail as Ursula and I grabbed our drag bags and costumes.

"Girl, you are gonna be Vicki all day and Raven all night for the next few days. Hope you don't get it twisted and start reciting prose when you should be twerking." Ursula laughed.

"I'm safe. I can't twerk." I replied acidly, stuffing some rhinestone heels into a bag. "My ass has never been able to jiggle that fast. But I *am* having a small identity crisis right now. There is too much going on, and I'm not keeping the car in between the lines."

"Oh, girl... Momma will soccer mom you if you start to careen off the road. Promise. I was a girl scout." Ursula beamed at me, a wicked gleam in her eye.

"Harper, you coming tonight?" Cory asked as he

fell onto my couch, looking exhausted.

"No. I have way too much to go over. I'm headed back to the office."

"All of the girls are coming tonight. Should be fun." Cory said without any energy.

"Unless someone dies." Ursula giggled. "Sorry, not funny. So, Domino was a bust, huh? I know you wanted it to be him." Ursula shook her head, making her afro sway back and forth with furiosity.

"It seems so. He's still an asshole, though." I ran into the dining room looking for a pair of earrings I was sure I stuffed into the drawer of my buffet. I kept china, wine glasses, and rhinestones in there. They all sparkled, so it made sense to me.

"You really think everyone is coming tonight?" I asked Cory, a very bad idea slapping me across the head.

"Sure. It's almost like a kick-off to the event, isn't it? I mean, the two of you on stage together is a big deal. They'll all be there." Cory cuddled up against the side of the couch. Poor sweet baby was beat.

I finished packing and made a decision. Ursula and I were about to become criminals.

"Those footprints at the door came back from the state with a little more information. They were Nike Shadows, and they still believe they were size twelve. The imprint was made from spilled face powder." Harper sat down his phone. "That's all they have, but at least it's more."

"Face powder? That could have been from any girl in the hotel that had to walk by that door, or even Lil' Debbie herself. Did you find any makeup residue in the room?" Ursula sipped her cocktail and watched me buzz around my house, straightening up. My house had become strewn with shit, and it was driving me crazy.

"Nothing. Her makeup was still packed in her bags." Harper pulled his feet up underneath him and rested his head on his hand. "Had to be from outside."

"But you didn't see any residue anywhere else?" I added. "If someone spilled a powder container out of their bag and it opened, it would have gotten over everything."

"No, it was just in that one spot where the shoe print was."

"Must have been a small spill, then." Cory shrugged. "Maybe from a small compact?"

"Maybe... That's possible, but drag queens don't use compacts very often. We prefer loose powder. It sets better." I threw a small pile of clothes on top of my washer.

"Drag 101, baby." Ursula agreed. "Child, will you stop puttering? You're making me more nervous than going to a high-school reunion."

I laughed and stuck out my tongue at her.

"The footprint had to come from somewhere in the Beach View Motel, doesn't it? I mean, it had to be close by." Ursula walked into the kitchen. "Y'all want a little coffee. Momma doesn't wanna fall asleep in the splits tonight, and that is a possibility."

"Yes, please." We all said in unison.

Ursula brewed coffee, and I walked in and pulled some mugs down for her. She shooed me away, and I went and cuddled up next to Cory. He wrapped his arm around me, and his breath tickled the top of my head.

I thought about my bad idea and formulated the plan Harper would never agree to. Keeping secrets is a good thing, right?

"You ou want to do what?" Cory looked at me like I had sprouted two heads. "Girl, that is cray-cray, and Harper would never..."

"That's why we can't tell Sheriff Hottie, isn't it?" I cut him off and continued contouring my face. "What do you think, Urs?"

"I think we're gonna commit a drag-felony tonight. Anything we can do to solve this case is something that needs to be done." She was way ahead of me and already putting on her eye shadow. "Did you bring flats?"

I chuckled. "No. But I did bring some tools that will help us get in. I had to learn how to pick locks while writing Murder in the Front Row. I'm quite good."

"Ooh! We're gonna be like the Bonnie and Cly...

Well, Bonnie and Bonnie of the breaking and entering club. I have my mace, just in case." She grinned wickedly. We were truly sisters.

"Cory, honey, you stay here and keep us updated on anyone who is staying at the Beach View. I know one room I want to get into, but are there any queens that have…" I jumped up from the mirror and walked over to where the queens had left their opening night costumes. I perused the shoes and looked for the girls that were staying at the same hotel as Lil' Debbie.

Eatta Twinkie had small heels, as did Valerie Rage. But Karen and Pam From Payroll wore King Kong heels. We would need to get into their rooms, too. I hated thinking of any of these girls as killers, but we couldn't afford to lose this opportunity. Here they were all in one place, and their rooms were empty. This was probably our only chance.

"Cory, who else is staying at the Beach View? Do you have your list?" I turned and smiled widely at him. He looked like he wanted to call Harper and rat us out, but I knew he wouldn't. He was ride or die.

He reached into his bag and pulled out his folder. "The dancers for Lil' Debbie and her stylists are there."

"Check. Small feet." I nodded. "Go on."

"Valerie Rage's dancers and her sponsor. They are staying in two separate rooms." He looked up at me.

"Well, we're checking out Domino's room for sure. But the dancer's feet were not that big, and they didn't know her at all. Next."

"Carson is staying with Pam in the same room. Then Joey has a room there, too."

"Hmm... Pam's room is already on the list. Can you write those room numbers down for me, hon?" I sat back down and covered my contour with a light base.

"You want me to keep them here for as long as I can, and what? Text you if any of them decide to go back to the hotel?" The color drained out of his face. This made him nervous, and I could understand why, but it still needed to be done.

"Yeah. It's what, a seven-minute walk to the hotel? Maybe ten if they're taking their time. That gives us plenty of time to get out and not be seen." I shrugged.

"Oh, yeah. Two fierce drag queens would never be noticed creeping around a small-town hotel." Cory laughed. "This is a bad idea, Vic."

I turned and winked at him. "Honey, I am full of them."

We finished getting ready, and by eight, the show began. Ursula and I each performed a couple numbers, and then a few of my other girls from the bar kept the party going. They were annoyed that they weren't allowed in the dressing room because of the pageant. But they showed up. We had thirty minutes before the show would be over, and Cory gave us a thumbs up.

Ursula and I snuck out of the bar and headed off to the motel in our smallest heels.

Chapter Thirteen

"**I** thought you said you were good at this," Ursula whispered loudly. The Motel was quiet, thank God, and there was no one around.

"Bitch, please. It's only been a minute, girl." I hissed as I felt my pick finally connect with the mechanism. "Turn the handle."

Ursula's shaking hand reached out, and with her turn, the door swung open.

"Told you I could do it," I whispered, glancing over our shoulder.

"Never had a doubt, ho." She stepped inside, and I followed, closing the door swiftly behind us.

Karen's room sat in darkness. I pulled out my flashlight and shown it around the incredibly messy room. Dresses hung from hangers, and clothes were strewn everywhere. Ursula's flashlight from her phone lit up, and bathed the room. Our double beams swept around as we searched for something, anything to shed some light on the case.

No box of poison sat on the table. There wasn't a receipt for a snake sitting on the bed. And even though there were a pair of tennis shoes, they were not Nike's. We opened the closet, and a suitcase tumbled out, spilling its contents onto the floor.

"Shit," I whispered. I stuffed the clothes back into the case and pushed it back. The closet was filled with drag and nothing else.

"She looks clean… Strike that. This bitch is messy as hell, but I don't see anything that says she's a killer. Just a hot mess." Ursula walked back towards the door. "Look at this dress. It's pretty."

"Girl, we are not shopping." I chuckled and glanced out through the window. "Looks clear."

We shut the door behind us and made sure to check that it was locked. Let's not make it any easier for whoever is after the girls. I adjusted my gloves, and we crept around to the next room. This one overlooked the small pool and belonged to Pam and Carson.

I pulled out my pick, and Ursula stood sentinel as I bent down and got to work. Crap… This one was more of a pain than the last one. My pick couldn't find the small metal edge. It had to be there…

"Girl, someone's…"

"Got it." It clicked, and Ursula and I fell inside, barely shutting the door before we heard the sound of heels on the concrete walkway. We held our breath, hoping that it wasn't Pam. I tried to remember if she had come to the club in drag or not, some of the girls did, and some didn't. I couldn't remember.

Ursula reached down and grabbed my hand as the shoes grew louder and passed by our door. We stood against it beginning to sweat. Their clicks faded, eventually. Both of us let out the breath we had been holding.

"I almost pissed myself," I sighed. We lit our lights and started exploring the room.

Pam's room was organized and meticulous except for the sink and mirror. Tubes and glass-covered plastic spilled onto the floor in piles. She brought an entire store of high-end makeup with her. There on the counter was makeup residue.

I shined my flashlight onto the floor.

"Urs. She spilled some powder." I glanced around the room. The beds were made, and new towels had been placed. That meant the room had been cleaned, which meant this powder was from today. So, she was messy. Every girl in this competition had loose powder, and it was incredibly easy to spill. The dressing room at the club was always covered in a fine sheen of it.

"The room has been cleaned," Ursula responded after a minute. She was sifting through the closet. "I don't see any tennis shoes besides these Converse. She brought a ton of heels, though."

Something struck me as odd. There was something

missing in this room... Something that I should notice easily.

I walked back towards the suitcases and opened one. This one had pantyhose and bras in it. The next had t-shirts and jeans. A carefully folded female top that she wouldn't be wearing at the pageant. Maybe it's something she would wear after. Maybe she would stay in drag and have a cocktail in it? Whatever, it belonged to Pam. That meant this suitcase did too.

"Urs? Do you see a suitcase or anything that might belong to Carson? He's staying here with Pam. At least, that's what Cory said." I shined my light under the beds. It was a double, so that made sense, but I could see no sign of Carson living here, too.

"There's a suit in the closet. I mean, it could belong to Pam, but... Why? Must be Carson's," she replied. "What's this?"

She pulled out a plastic bag and glanced inside. "Nothing... Just dirty clothes."

"Shouldn't he have a suitcase? He's here for a week." I said, confused by the lack of evidence of his living here.

"There's a duffel. It's empty, though. Did you look in the drawers? Carson is a Kween with a capital K."

I opened a drawer, and sure enough, there were some folded clothes that belonged to a man. They looked like the kind of clothes Carson would wear – expensive. A pair of cowhide shoes, size thirteen, sat in one of the drawers, but there were no tennis shoes.

Carson wasn't really a tennis shoe guy. He liked designer clothes. Carson saw himself as an A-Gay. In San Diego, he was. But it was too staged. It just didn't feel right. He was here for a week, and this is all he brought?

I sifted through the drawers and found nothing. Well, the shoe was close to the right size, but after interviewing him... He knew Lil' Debbie better than everyone else and seemed genuinely upset at his death.

"Nothing here, child. You ready to go to Domino's?" Ursula placed her hand on my shoulder, and I damn near jumped out of my heels.

"Yeah. I guess. Pam and Carson seem clean, even if both of them wear the right size. It would be a stretch for them to be involved. Pam's already one of the favorites."

I peeked out the window and paused at the door listening for any shoes headed our way. It was quiet, and we slowly cracked the door and peered out.

"Looks good. Let's go." Ursula breathed in my ear.

We shut the door behind us and walked away, acting like we belonged there just in case we hit some pedestrian traffic. We didn't. We walked quickly and as quietly as we could around the corner and up the stairs to Domino's room. I glanced where we were and noticed that we were not far from the room where Lil' Debbie was murdered. Her room was just a few doors down and on the bottom floor.

I glanced around and saw no one. Ursula stood in front of me, blocking me from view as I crouched down and started working on his lock. Doing this with Ursula felt dangerous and exciting. Just having her here bolstered me enough that I felt safer than I should. She was a big woman, and I knew she could take care of herself.

Domino's lock came open faster than the others, and I slowly turned the handle. The light from the TV flickered across the room, but it was quiet inside. Cory would text me if he left. I knew that.

We shut the door behind us and turned on our lights. I started at the front of the room, and Ursula moved to the rear. I heard her moving things around. Domino's computer was open, and I pressed the CTRL button numerous times to see if it would pop on. Surprisingly, it did.

I knelt in front of it and was surprised to find it unlocked. That was too easy. I looked at the tabs that were open at the bottom and found an excel spreadsheet with all of the contestant's names on their own tabs. It was a list of each strength and weakness that he perceived them to have. Some notes written to the side explained the list. Judy had a rather large list of strengths and weaknesses. So did Pam and Eatta. I clicked on Lil' Debbie, and it was blank.

Interesting...

I clicked his Explorer tab that was open, and lo and behold... His email was open, and for fuck sakes, he used Hotmail. Maybe there was email correspondence between him and Lil' Debbie?

I put her name in the search bar, and nothing came up. That was surprising. I tried Barry and watched the computer's spinning wheel of death as it searched.

Two emails finally came up, and I clicked on one. Thinking of moving to San Francisco, here's my cell number. Can we talk, yadda yadda... Nothing.

I clicked on the other one. It was about the same thing, but here he talked about the guy he was dating and how he would be mad if he chose to go to San Francisco instead of where he was at. I kept reading... Nothing. No name, no city... Come on, Barry. Help a bitch out.

My phone vibrated, and I quickly pulled it out. My eyes bugged out of my head.

"Ursula... We gotta go, now."

"Shit! Why?" She whispered loudly.

"Cory has lost sight of Domino. He doesn't see him in the bar and doesn't know when he left."

I canceled my search and shut the laptop before going to peer out the window and gasping at what I saw.

"Girl! Now!" I said much louder than I intended. I shut my flashlight off and went to the door and cracked it, peering through. I felt Ursula put her hand on my shoulder. "He's crossing the street. We need to wait until he gets close enough that he can't see us, and then we need to book it to the right and to the far corner. Yeah... He's headed to the staircase on the other side. Ready?"

Ursula patted me. "Shit. I was born ready."

"Let's go!" We ran out the door, and I quickly and as quietly as I could shut it behind us. We took off like a bat out of hell. I reached down and pulled my shoes off, and Ursula damn near knocked me down as she brushed by me. I wanted to hide the telltale clicks of women running away from committing a felony. My breastplate bouncing and knocking me off-kilter as I ran behind her. We practically skidded around the corner, and I glanced carefully back to see Domino slowly ascending the stairs as he stared at his phone.

We did it. But what did it accomplish?

He was in contact with Lil' Debbie, and she mentioned a boyfriend. But that was it—no other information to help me. Then Ursula whispered in my ear.

"He had a pair of tennis shoes, girl, and I think they were Nike's."

Chapter Fourteen

*H*arper was pissed.

Like, really pissed.

His boyfriend committed a felony and then told him about it, thereby making him an accomplice.

Pissed.

"So, you thought you should break into their rooms and search through their belongings..."

"and Domino's computer," Cory added, and I threw a pillow at him, shooting a warning in his direction.

"Yes. Thank you, Cory. Go through their personal stuff without a warrant? You know that if you had found anything..."

"It couldn't have been used. Yes, I know. But we would have known." I said forcibly, and Harper stood up and walked away. "Then you would have been able to ask the right questions, and you could have found the evidence correctly."

"You know how insane this sounds, right? If you had been caught..."

"We weren't," I shouted louder than I intended. "And I know it was... not legal, Harper, but I felt like I had to do something, and you couldn't do this... So, we did."

"Ursula, I can't believe you went along with this." Harper ran his fingers through his hair and threw himself back into the chair.

"Boo... I am always willing to walk in the grey if it helps us figure out the truth. One of our girls has died, and as her sisters, we are willing to do what has to be done. We weren't caught, and we told you about it, which I admit might not have been the best idea. But at least we didn't lie. My husband would be pissed, too, promise. But what's done is done, and we know more than we did before." Ursula said seriously and slowly.

"Not much," I added. "But something. She had a boyfriend who would not be happy if she moved to San Francisco, yet she was still planning on it."

"Great. So more mysteries and no answers." Cory groaned.

"You're not helping, boo." I laughed. "We also found tennis shoes in Domino's hotel room."

"Shocking." Harper rolled his eyes. "Were they Nike Shadows?"

"They were tennis shoes. As soon as I found them, we had to skedaddle, hon. I don't know." Ursula shrugged. "I think I saw the swoosh, but it could have been something else. It was dark, hon."

"So we know he wears shoes, and sometimes they are comfortable ones. Not to mention, I checked Domino's GPA with his company, and his car was indeed outside the city when the murder happened. I could have saved you a B and E charge if you had just let me know. Domino is not our guy. I know you're fixated on him, but..."

"I'm not." My defenses popped to the forefront. "Not really, I... He's not a very nice guy. If any of these people are a killer, it would be him."

"That's Vic talking and not Vicki, and you know it."

"I am the same person, Harper." I collapsed beside him. "Trust me. I know what we did was... I get it, ok? But I have a lead that I think I can follow in the drag community. It's at least something new, right?"

"I guess." He huffed and pulled me closer to him. I traced my fingers over his bright ink on his arm.

"Are you done being mad?" I said overly sweetly.

"I wasn't mad, Vic. Well, I was... But I was more... That was dangerous, or it could have been. If one of them really was..."

"Well, it doesn't look like they were, huh?"

"You are such a pain." He kissed my cheek, and Ursula burst out laughing.

"I'm going home. I'm exhausted." Cory announced and hugged us all goodbye.

I slept in Harper's arms, but all I could think about was those shoes in Domino's closet.

Chapter Fifteen

The next day was full of pageant work. The bar was getting spruced up, and the girls had their final rehearsals before they were released for the day. The opening number looked great, as did the other two. They brought their A-game and worked that stage like a stripper on a pole. It was fabulous. Even Karen and she had two large left feet.

After they left, Ursula and I headed home to grab our own stuff and grab some lunch before heading back. We had to meet the judges and give them the paperwork they would use to rank the contestants on this first night of the competition.

Tonight was one of my least favorite portions: business-wear and onstage interviews. The one thing I could be sure of is no one would answer a question with world peace, like most straight people beauty pageants. I always wanted to slap every girl on TV who used that as an answer to what do you most want in the world. It was a total cop-out. What she wanted was to be fabulously wealthy and happier than anyone else she knew. Pageant girls were all the same. They would cut a bitch faster than anyone.

We went back, drag bags in hand, and put our stuff in the small dressing room. The bar looked amazing, candle holders sat on the small tables, and the dance floor had even more small café tables added to accommodate as many people as possible. I was surprised to walk out and find Joey sitting at the bar.

"Hey, Joey. Why are you here so early?" I asked, making sure to be loud enough for Ursula to hear, just in case she decided to throw shade, thinking we were alone.

"Nerves, I guess. I get this way before every state final. Rehearsal looked great this morning." He seemed jittery. Well, he said he was nervous. Some people handled stress better than others. "The judges should be here around six, so I can take them out to dinner before the pageant. Would you or Ursula like to join us?"

"Uh... I think I have my hands full already. It's been a hell of a week."

"You can say that again. Has your boyfriend found any leads to who committed these crimes? Everyone's on edge around here wondering if they're gonna be next." He looked stricken, as if this whole drama was just too much for him. Not everyone handles murder well, and yes, I know how that sounds.

"I'm just a drag queen and a retired hairdresser, Joey. He doesn't discuss his cases with me." I lied.

"I just hope everything goes smoothly tonight. The national competition doesn't look kindly on dead contestants. This whole thing could blow up in my face." He whined. "I didn't... never mind. I'm just jumpy."

I did feel sorry for him. This was not what anyone signed up for, and he was in charge, albeit lazily, of the state competitions.

"I'm sure. I mean, no one has tried to hurt anyone in over twenty-four hours. That's a good sign." I tried to make him feel better but only succeeded in depressing myself. "Poor Lil' Debbie. The girls said she was really something."

"She was really a pain in the ass, but yeah, she was a fierce performer. Barry was a... He was a perfection- ist, and he demanded perfection from everyone. That included answering an email in what he considered to be a timely fashion. But to know he died... I mean, I would love to get another email from him, now." Joey mused, looking at the shelves behind the bar. "This has all been too much, Victor." He slumped onto the bar top, and I thought he might be about to burst into tears. I really needed him to hold it together.

"Did you know Barry that well? I knew nothing about him." I sat down beside him. "Did he have a boyfriend or anything? It just seems so sad if he didn't. Dying alone and... you know."

"He had an ex that's back in jail, and recently he started seeing someone. Barry would have been an insane boyfriend." Joey glanced at his watch. "Tomorrow is the talent run through with tech, right?"

"Yeah. Cory will be handling that." I shrugged.

"Well, I better answer some of these emails." Joey pulled out his computer, and I stood there for a second before walking away. I felt for him. I did. But whatever he was going through was his own journey, and I had mine. Right now, all I could think about was hoping we got through the night without an attempted murder. The odds were not on our side.

Joey met the judges and introduced me to them. They, of course, already knew Ursula and were excited to meet her. Most gays lost their minds when they met her. Her TV show really was that good. There was just something loving and compassionate about her like she was family. She handled them with flair and then sent them on their way to dinner with Joey, feigning being too busy to join them. Honestly, at this point, there was nothing we could do. Everything that could be prepared already was, and all that was left was to start this monster of a pageant and cross our fingers that we would survive it. Literally.

The girls started filing in one by one. It would be a busy night for them with many costume changes. The racks started filling up with gowns and business attire, as well as their opening costumes. Some of the girls entered in half drag, their faces looking garish from beginning their underpainting at the hotel. Judy arrived looking like a kabuki horror doll. I gasped when I saw her. It was drastic, and I was intrigued by what the final look would be.

The girls were all in a good mood, but gossip was not really on their minds. They kept to themselves and painted their faces while members of their teams steamed their garments and sprayed their hair in place on the wig heads that set all along the far wall. If someone had lit a match, that place would have exploded with the amount of hairspray in the air. You could taste it.

Ursula and I got into our evening gowns, and I looked at myself in my mirror and grinned. She zipped me up, and I had to suck my stomach in to get it to fasten. I needed to watch out, or I wasn't going to fit in my dresses much longer. I hadn't been very active since I've been trying to finish the next book. Sitting and writing made me have more junk in my trunk. I kind of liked it. Harper did too.

The citizens of Maple Bay were filling up the bar and chattering and drinking as they waited for the show to begin. I glanced out the curtain and saw Harper sitting with Jensen and Betty Davis and slapped myself in the head.

Shit! Vicki Dean was supposed to make an appearance. I didn't bring her with me, and I made a mental note that tomorrow night, Ursula and I would have to find a way for Vicki to be seen. It was the talent portion of the competition tomorrow night, and even if I did have to MC the event, maybe Urs and I could portion it out so Vicki could at least make an appearance towards the end of the night. If I didn't find a way, Betty would never let me live it down.

I heard from Cory that she said on air, this pageant was as exciting as it was deadly. She had, of course, been talking about the murder of Lil' Debbie and how the sheriff's department had no leads. She loved to spread bad news, and yes, I did know it was her job. But that didn't mean she had to be so gleeful about it. I swear you would think she thought murder was good PR for this town.

"You ready? Cory just waved at me and gave me five til places." Ursula placed her large hand on my shoulder.

It was time. Cory came back from the back room, and the girls began to file out in some of the most hideous costumes I had ever seen. We had a bridge, a sequoia, a bottle of wine, the Hollywood sign, and I think the Joshua Tree, but I wasn't really sure. Judy's costume was surprising and maybe the most artistic. She was the letters of the Zodiac killer. She looked terrifying, and I finally realized why she was one of the most admired girls in the pageant. She was unique and totally unlike any of the others.

The lights went down, and the music started blaring. Cory's voice boomed out over the speakers.

"Ladies and laddies who wanna be ladies, welcome to the thirteenth Ms. Cali West Coast Pageant here at our very own Maple Bay gay bar, Rumors. Sit back and relax as our contestants honor the great state we all live in. Get ready to break a nail cause these girls have come to slay and not play. I present to you the contestants vying for the crown. Ladies... Take it away."

Katy Perry's California Gurls started playing, and our ladies took the stage, making a criss-cross pattern as they entered, giving the audience a good look at their drag. The crowd applauded as each entered, and Ursula and I crossed our fingers as they began the choreography. The song morphed into Judy Garland singing San Francisco and then into Sheryl Crow's, All I Wanna Do. It ended finally with The Beach Boys' California Girls - almost like a bookend. It was a horrible medley, and I hated it as soon as I heard it, but it's what the state pageant put together.

The girls did great, and not one of them fumbled onstage. They were pros and pulled it together, and when they struck the last pose, they held it for just a second before the crowd burst into applause.

They all used their hand closest to the center of the stage and gestured to where we would enter. Cory's voice boomed again, and I clutched the microphone in my hand.

"Ladies and Laddies who wanna be ladies, cause

here aren't we all drag queens? Your hostess with the mostess, Ms. Raven Ravonne."

I stepped out from the center of the curtain, feeling like a rhinestone and ruby fantasy. I dripped opulence, and as soon as the spotlight caught me onstage, I glowed with an unearthly gemstone realness that dazzled everyone. At least that's how I saw it.

"Biiiiitch!" I said as deeply as I could, and the crowd laughed. "Let's hear it for these ladies, once again. Our own California divas vying for a crown that doesn't sparkle nearly as much as this evening gown does." The audience clapped again, and the girls all bowed and exited as gracefully as a barge can. Seriously their costumes barely fit through the damn curtain.

"You like this old thing? Isn't it pretty? I feel like I just robbed the crown jewels and superglued them onto myself. You know how we drag queens are. You invite us over to dinner, and we leave with your silverware shoved up our cooch. We like things that sparkle, and darlings I am incandescent tonight." I spun onstage and looked out into the crowd.

A few catcalls and whistles made me grin. "Keep it up... keep it up, boys. Momma likes them right out of college and full of muscles, so who's gonna get lucky tonight?"

"Probably the sheriff!" Jensen said loudly, and the crowd laughed.

"Honey, he already got lucky. He woke up to this,

this morning." I winked, and the crowd laughed again. "Trust... It ain't pretty at six in the morning. She's got a beard."

"So who is here to see our contestants battle it out on stage. My money is on the big one because this contest ends with a boxing match. Hey, guess what?" I made a big gesture with my hand and cupped my ear. The audience knew what to do.

"What!" They bellowed back to me.

"I'm not alone today. I have a co-host, and we're splitting the stage the way I split my panties earlier. You wanna know who it is? She's a big... big star. She's on TV..." The crowd clapped. "Maple Bay, I give you the one and only, the most fabulous diva who ever diva'd – Ms. Ursula Moolay."

Ursula stepped out in a black velvet gown with puffy shoulders and a small train. Rhinestones twinkled from the bottom and the bust of the dress as she slinked onto the stage and towards me, giving me a big kiss.

"You all wanna see us kai-kai?" Ursula laughed, and the crowd clapped. "Of course, you do. Perverts."

"Ursula, you look ravishing. All that body-ody-ody, baby."

"Raven, your husband looks ravishing." The crowd burst into laughter again. "Just kidding, momma. You look... good."

"Yeah?"

"Yeah."

The music came on, and Ursula and I lip-synced to Angela Lansbury and Bea Arthur's version of Bosom Buddies from Mame. The crowd ate it up, and we over-acted until we were about to burst into laughter ourselves – one-upping each other and emoting our asses off. It was one of the most fun times I had ever had on stage, and the joy on our faces was not fake. This shit was fun.

We ended, and the crowd erupted into applause again.

"So tonight is the first night of our three-night extravanganza special event."

Ursula looked at me and laughed. "I think it's more of a mini-series."

"What do you mean?"

"It's two nights too long." The crowd laughed again. "Tonight is the interview and businesswoman realness portion of the competition. In case these ladies decide to get a job as a high-powered secretary. Maybe even a CEO if they're smart. But I've met these girls, so I know better."

"I prefer to call it, Dynasty realness. Alexis Carrington Colby was my idol in those business power suits." I said smugly.

"I was Dominique Devereaux, all the way, baby. Black girl magic."

We bantered for a little longer and kept the audience laughing while the girls got into their business attire. Cory gave us the thumbs up, and we began the competition.

"Alright, Maple Bay, here are the ladies who lunch. We're starting off with Pam From Payroll."

Pam walked out onstage wearing a pink glittered two-piece business suit. She walked to the center of the stage and popped the buttons on her jacket, slowly pulling it off to reveal a sheer pink top with a black bra underneath. The crowd ate it up, and she played the stage, working every inch of it in her pink stilettos.

We announced the other contestants. Pussina was next, and she was dazzling, with another big reveal to her costume that made the audience applaud and ooh and aah. Eatta Twinkie followed her in a metal suit that looked like a work of art. It had spray-painted graffiti on the back of the jacket, which also had wires dangling from it like fringe.

Shae Black and Dammit Janet were the next two girls, and their ensembles were boring compared to what we had already seen. Tapered and sleek but pedestrian compared to the ones who had come before.

Karen had a suit made of copy paper that she tore off little pieces from. It was form-fitting, and she peeled it off, piece by piece until she stood there in another suit made from the slick paper covers that copy paper came in. It was magical.

Valerie Rage walked onto the stage in a pair of heels that defied gravity. She was so tall, she had to duck under the curtain. Her suit was fabulous and cost more than a house, I was sure. It was Gucci and had the label all over it, so you couldn't miss it. Nice, yes. Amazing and inventive, no.

I almost fell off the stage when Judy Ghouland walked out. She was zombified and ghoulish, her flesh literally peeling off her body in a small suit made from duct tape and paper clips. I was in shock. She peeled pieces of her flesh off and flung them out into the audience, who clamored to grab them. She was that thing that all the other girls dreamed of – one of a kind.

Our Maple Bay girl was next, and the audience clapped louder for her than anyone else. Vivienne took the stage, looking like power. She wore a large robe that looked like it was made out of large checks. She spun around, and debt dripped in red lettering like blood. She slowly dropped the robe, and her dress was made out of dollar bills. Even her stockings looked like they were made of money. She looked fabulous, and I smiled with pride. That was my girl.

Ursula and I performed another number and continued our bad jokes to the audience, who now were feeling no pain. We gave the girls enough time to finish their change, and we began the interview portion of the competition. Each girl was asked two questions, and they all did quite well. Vivienne surprised us again, though. She brought trans rights to the forefront of her answers and sounded the most intelligent out of all of them. She was incredibly smart.

She had a master's degree. Shit, I barely finished high school.

Ursula and I did one final number and thanked them all for coming, as well as reminding them that tomorrow night was the talent portion of the pageant.

When we walked off stage, the girls were all changing clothes and putting their drag away. We also changed clothes and wiped our stage personas off. Well, I wiped mine off. Ursula really was Ursula all the time since she realized her true identity. I was just a boy in a dress who liked to lip-sync to divas. I slipped into my t-shirt and jeans and headed home.

I think we all slept like a baby.

Chapter Sixteen

Harper woke me up with a nudge. I rolled over.

"How fast can you change into Vicki?"

"Right now?" I groaned. "Why? That's just mean."

"I have Lil' Debbie's sponsor from Long Beach sitting in the station, according to Carpenter. She wants to talk to me." He said huskily, his breath all minty fresh. "I just got off the phone. Hurry up, I made coffee."

"God, I hate morning people. Give me... fifteen minutes. I'll paint quickly and wear glasses, I guess. Jesus... How fast can you get into drag? Those words leave chills down a drag queen's back."

I was still applying makeup as we drove into town. I texted Cory and asked him to pick me up at the station in an hour. Bless his heart, he texted back, even if it was nine in the morning. I know he had a late night. I saw him and Joey in deep conversation. They were cute, but I hoped Cory knew what he was doing. He had a fragile heart.

Harper pulled into his parking spot, and I barely got finished beating my face enough to be seen in public, from a distance, with glasses and a hat on. Maybe? God, I hoped so because it was happening right now, and I had perhaps the least makeup on I've ever had in my life.

I would have preferred to have this conversation with Lil' Debbie's sponsor when I was more awake and put together. Perhaps Heather decided to make an appearance at the event but decided not to stay?

We got out of Harper's truck and walked in through the back door of the station. A few of the guys waved at us, and I headed into his office. Harper walked up to the front to meet Heather. I pulled one of the chairs around as far away from where she would be sitting. I needed the distance so she wouldn't clock that Vicki Dean was a man.

Harper entered, followed by a short woman with a buzzcut. She looked like she hadn't slept in a while, the dark circles under her eyes a marker to her mourning. She nodded at me as she took a seat, looking uncomfortable and edgy. She shifted her position and crossed her ankles as she slid her feet under the chair.

"Heather Campion, this is Vicki Dean. She's been working with us on Barry's case." Harper's voice was rough. He was as tired as I was. If this case didn't end soon, it was going to take an even harsher toll on us.

"Ms. Dean." She stood and offered her hand. She had a very strong handshake for such a little thing. She sat back down in the same position and took a breath. The look on her face told me that she had something she needed to get off her chest.

"Ms. Campion... Heather, do you mind if I call you that?" She nodded her agreement. "Carpenter said you wanted to talk to us about the case. You were in Long Beach, correct?"

"Yeah... I hate leaving the bar for long periods of time. I was planning on being here to watch Lil' Debbie on the first night and stay through the end of the event. Instead, I have decided to head back to Long Beach later today, if you have no problem with that. It's too hard to stay here and watch. Barry was a bull-headed asshole, but he was my bullheaded asshole, and I can't believe that... I've been in shock since I found out." She looked back and forth between us.

"I can understand that," I said sympathetically. This was as hard as all the other interviews. Lying to my LGBT sisters and brothers, my drag sisters, when all I wanted to do was tell them how much I under-stood. How I knew how hard they worked for this moment and how sad it was to have it ripped away so violently.

"I wanted to tell you... You may already know what I'm about to tell you. Maybe you don't. But Barry was leaving Long Beach. He really wanted a new start after everything that happened between him and his ex."

"Is this the man who's currently in prison?" Harper's question made her frown.

She looked at him and nodded before sighing. "I can't believe I will never argue with him again, even if he was leaving me to start somewhere all over again. I understood why. Barry had a rough go of it, and he wanted to leave all of that behind him."

"Do you think his ex may have had anything to do with his death?" I asked carefully. Was this what she was implying?

"I don't see how. I mean, he had no idea about Barry leaving, as far as I know. He's been in prison for a while, and I know Barry wasn't communicating with him. No, I don't think Jack had anything to do with Barry's death. I think this was an act of anger for a totally different reason."

"Ok..." Harper nodded and glanced over at me. "Go on."

"Barry was looking for a new place to live, and he had decided between a few cities with a thriving drag scene. He had reached out to the pageant community in order to find a new sponsor. He had all but decided to move to San Francisco, and... How much do you know about the drag world?" She asked suddenly, and I had to stifle my grin.

"We have friends who are involved. My boyfriend is

the drag queen who is hosting the pageant." Harper said proudly. I wanted to reach over and kiss him.

"I see... Raven was a well-known Frisco queen, so I'm sure she knew the seedy underside of the bar scene. But she wasn't a pageant girl. Neither was Ursula Moolay, really. Besides, with her reality stardom, she's in a class of her own. The pageant world is full of backstabbing and doing whatever it takes to win. These girls have to have a very thick skin, but most of the... drama is behind the scenes with people like me. The people who spend a ton of money to bring a crown back to their hometown bar. It's a lot of work and an investment, both in cash and time that we all put into our queens."

She leaned forward and scooted her chair a little closer to the desk. "The pageant system has a hierarchy, just like anything else. Think of it as being promoted from within. You put in your time and compete enough... If you keep getting better and compete at a high level for enough years, eventually you are the runner up, then if things go as expected, you win. Lil' Debbie was one of those queens that would be the next in line to rise up the system's ladder in the next few years. She was a fierce competitor, and this was not going to be her year, probably. But if Pam or Judy won, she may have been second or the first runner up next year. Which means..."

"She was in line to be a champion. I see. So having her as one of your queens would have been something that all of the various sponsors would have wanted?" I answered, understanding it better than I ever had, thanks to her.

"Exactly. Barry had settled on going to San Francisco, and then something changed his mind. I hated him moving, but I couldn't be mad at him. I just don't know why he suddenly decided to go someplace else. I don't know where. I'm sorry. I know he was dating a guy off and on from San Diego, and that was a possibility for a while, but I think if he had chosen to move there, I would have known."

"So, you know Domino?" I asked carefully. She nodded and grimaced. "I take it you are not a fan?"

"No. He's everything that's wrong with gay bars and drag pageants. I know he wanted Barry and was willing to offer him whatever he needed to join him. Domino wouldn't take being told no, easily."

"He did tell us about his conversations with Barry. Supposedly he was going to be told what Barry had decided here at the pageant."

"I can't answer that. Maybe he already knew, or maybe Barry wanted to wait to tell him, I don't know. But he told me that he didn't trust Domino. Sorry, that's all I know."

"When did you find out that Barry was leaving?" There was something here in what she was telling us. I just couldn't find the thread to unravel it yet.

"I've known for a couple months. He came to the bar and told me that he needed to start over. He waited until this pageant was over, though, because if he did win, so did I, and that would be good for the bar and whatever girl I decided to take on next. At first, he wanted to take off right then, but I begged him to wait, and he did. He knew he owed me that. Is that all? I really would like to get back to Long Beach before it gets dark if possible."

Harper walked Heather out and got all of her information.

Everything still pointed to Domino to me. Now all I had to do was find what he was hiding.

I heard my phone buzz in my bag, and I pulled it out.

"Cory? I was just about to call you." I grinned.

"I'm on my way to get you. We gotta get you home and de-Vicki you as quick as we can. Raven got a phone call from an old friend who just heard about Lil' Debbie's murder."

"Ok... what are we doing?" I asked, perplexed and surprised by the new info."

"Girl, you and Ursula are going to the mecca. Car trip to San Francisco. Meet me outside in five."

Couldn't we just talk to her on the phone?

Chapter Seventeen

*D*rag queens always make things too damn difficult.

Cory picked me up and broke speed records as he drove me back home to de-drag and throw on some boy clothes. He had to be at the bar for the girl's talent technical rehearsals today. They each had thirty minutes to check lighting cues and move any set pieces on and off the stage before the second night of the competition. He was pissy that we had to leave him behind. My bestie really wanted to go with us and pouted. It was adorable.

Ursula and I took off for San Fran, knowing that this had to be a fast trip. We had to be back and get ready to MC the event tonight. We had a little over six hours before we had to be back. That meant I needed to drive like there was a sale at Macy's. It was practically a two-hour trip one way.

"How do you know this person again?" I asked as I flew past a girl who drove like my grandma.

"Well, I called a few of my contacts in San Fran to see if Lil' Debbie had been in contact with any of them. They all said no but would ask around, and this morning I got a text from Ms. Piggy Stardust. Do you know her?" Ursula reached over and turned the radio down.

"By name. She's been around forever, but I don't think we ever worked together. I know a couple of her daughters, though." I had heard of her. She was the mother to many legendary queens in the city. Ms. Piggy Stardust was one of those girls that everyone loved. She had been around so long she was almost royalty.

"Well, one of her daughters, Permadette Peters, had moved here from San Diego and knew Lil' Debbie when she lived down there. Apparently, they had been in contact, and she was expecting her to move into her empty room for a while until she could find her own place. So maybe she knows something else."

"Interesting. Why couldn't we talk to her on the phone? We're gonna be cutting this super close, and I still have to figure out how Vicki can watch part of the pageant tonight." I huffed. That had been worrying me. If Betty didn't see me, she would talk about it on the radio, and if she talked about it... People might start wondering why. Any kind of suspicion could eventually lead them to Vicki and Victor being the same person if they looked hard enough.

"Oh, child... Permadette pays for her minutes and didn't want to use them talking to us." She cackled. "But I thought about your Vicki dilemma this morning. I knew you were worried about it. Vicki likes to wear hats, doesn't she?" Ursula told me her plan, and it was weird and wacky enough that it might actually work. I would have to think about it and see if it was something I could manage. Thank the drag gods that Ursula could pull some of the MC duties away from me. That would help.

We crossed the bridge and made good time. Thankfully she lived on Geary, so we wouldn't have to drive through the city. I turned right and started driving up and down the hills of the place I used to call home. Well, I didn't live anywhere near here. I lived further south near Castro. I had always liked living in the heart of everything, and Gayville was what I enjoyed back then.

I found parking, miraculously, a few blocks away and somehow remembered how to parallel park on the side of what felt like a mountain. Ursula and I both tumbled from my car and somehow prevented ourselves from rolling downhill. I had forgotten how hard this was.

"Lord, child! I love to visit this place, except for the smell of weed that is just every fucking where. I have never liked that very much. You just can't escape it up here. But I do not know how you people can park on hills like this. I would be terrified." Ursula laughed as she waited for me to get up onto the cracked sidewalk. In San Fran, we rarely fixed them because they were just gonna crack again at the next earthquake. You got used to it.

"Yeah. I still don't like it. It's been a while since I lived here, remember? That is not like getting back on a bike, sis. I may have said a silent prayer when I put the car in reverse." I looked up the hill. "According to the address, it's three blocks up this hill."

"You have got to be... Shit." Ursula grabbed my hand, and we helped each other up the steep sidewalk. "This would be another reason I couldn't live here. Momma don't like to work out when she's just trying to get to brunch. Damn."

"It takes a special kind of person to live in the Babylon by the Bay. There's an old saying that everyone who comes here and falls in love with the city has been reincarnated and once lived on Atlantis."

"The city that sunk into the ocean. I thought that was where Aquaman lived." Ursula laughed.

"There's a lot of people who think the gay mecca was built over the ruins of Atlantis. It's true... I mean the persisting belief... not that it's real. I will say this, though... Most of the people who love it here were lost in their former lives and didn't feel truly at home until they moved here. It's fun mythology if nothing else." I was starting to breathe hard. So was Urs.

"Why did you... move away if this was... where you belonged? Damn, this is steep as shit."

"I never said I belonged. This was just a stop for me to find Maple Bay. I knew as soon as I visited that it was where I was supposed to be. You, ok?"

"Two more blocks?" She nodded.

"Yeah... Two more blocks."

We remained silent as we trudged up the hill, thankful that we were in flats. Walking up these hills sucked but walking down them was downright treacherous. Our breathing became more labored, and by the time we got to Permadette's building, we were both trying to catch our breath.

"Number... four," she said, trying to pull in a deep breath. Ursula sat down on the stoop and looked like she might pass out.

I pressed the button and heard a ringing from one of the upstairs windows. Most of the windows were wide open, letting in a breeze on this beautiful day. I heard the ringing stop.

"Hey! You must be Ursula and Raven?" A deep voice answered. For a second, I thought it was coming out of the box, and then I glanced up. Permadette, I assumed, waved at us from the window. "Hold on, girls. I'll be right down."

Ursula wiped some perspiration off her forehead with a small kerchief she pulled out of her bag. She dabbed herself and slid the rag back into her bag.

"There's a café across the street. I could use an iced tea or something."

The door opened and out walked a short man with a healthy beer gut—his bright red hair was as curly and kinky as the cartoon character Annie. Now I got the name... "Hey girls, we can go up to my place. It's very nice to meet you. I'm a huge fan, Ursula."

"That's sweet, boo. This place have an elevator?" Ursula said deeply, still breathing harder than I currently was.

"No elevator. Just the stairs." Permadette shut the door behind her.

"Then pumpkin... I think we should jaywalk and go to that café over there. I already climbed a mountain, and momma can't do stairs right now. My treat, come on." Ursula stood and took a deep breath. "I don't know how you queens live here. If I were in heels, I would have broken my damn neck."

We played Frogger crossing the street and sat down at one of the small tables outside. A waitress took our coffee and tea orders and went back inside, leaving us to stare at each other.

"Permadette Peters... Cute name. You wear your own hair or..." Ursula mimed Bernadette Peters's long hair, and Permadette laughed.

"Oh no. This is my natural hair, but I wear a wig. I couldn't get my hair that big. It really is a pleasure to meet you. Mother Stardust talks highly of you. Raven, I know we don't know each other, but I work at your old bar. They still talk about how sickening you were."

"That's sweet. I'm surprised any of my old girl-friends still work there. So, you knew Lil' Debbie. Did you know her well?" I asked politely, concerned that they were friends.

"Right to it, huh?" Permadette laughed. "Oh, you have to get back for the pageant. Oh yeah… Barry and I were friendly. We knew each other from the bar scene in San Diego. I was there for the first night he performed, even. But we weren't really close. He wasn't one of my best Judy's, or anything like that. But we hung in the same circles. Hard to believe he's dead. If Pussina hadn't told Amber and she hadn't told Monique, Mother Stardust wouldn't have known to tell me." His face fell. "Shit, I may have been waiting for him to arrive and never knew why he didn't."

"We have heard a lot of rumors and hearsay about Barry's decision to leave Long Beach and move. Some people think he was coming here, and others think he had changed his mind. When was the last time you spoke to him?" Ursula reached over and patted Permadette's hand.

"Oh, that's easy. I saw him the morning he died. He stopped here and dropped off a check for his first four month's rent before driving up to Maple Bay. I was surprised he paid so far in advance with everything he told me, you know? I cashed it before I… Well, you do know. If I had known this shit was going to happen, I wouldn't have. It feels like I stole something now."

"Four months rent... Damn. You should consider that a gift, hon. By yourself a new dress as a way to remember his memory. I'm sure he would love that."

"Shit...Mmm..." He growled. "You didn't know Barry, did you?" Permadette laughed. "He would have wanted every dollar back to take to his grave. Barry was tighter than my perm with his cash. Always has been because he never had anything. He was going to declare bankruptcy after his move. I don't think he had much of a choice, really. He seemed a little ashamed of that."

"That far in debt, huh? Well, he can't ask for it back, now. Do what Ursula suggests. Wear it and be fierce for her. So, you saw him that morning, and he was moving to San Francisco... This just got..."

"Well, he changed his mind a couple of times as a girl is want to do, you know? A few months ago, he called me and wanted to move. Then it was, I have to wait until this pageant is over. But then he started dating this guy from San Diego. All of a sudden, he was planning on moving there and was incredibly excited about it. He said I knew him, and I would lose my mind if he told me who it was. Of course, that bitch never did. Instead, I got a message two weeks ago asking if he could still stay here. Things didn't work out the way he thought they would. I said yes, and she showed up this week with a check. I couldn't believe she had that kind of money saved up. It was a little over four thousand dollars."

The waitress finally brought our drinks, and Ursula put the straw in her mouth and sipped the shit out of her iced tea. By the time Permadette and I had taken a sip, Ursula was sucking air in her straw.

"I was thirsty, bitch." She pursed her lips and rolled her neck at me. "Hon?" She flagged down the waitress. "Do you mind?"

"That is a lot of money for someone who was about to declare bankruptcy. Do you know anything else about this guy she dated?"

"Well, I know I knew him, according to her. Girl, I knew everybody, so that don't help no one. But I do know that whatever happened between them was pretty bad. She was really upset over it. Said he wasn't who he pretended to be, and she wasn't gonna be able to shake him for a while, even if she wasn't with him. Whatever that means. Poor old thing suffered more than Saint Whitney when it came to men. Always did. Barry had shit taste in guys."

"Wasn't gonna be able to shake him? What does that mean?" Ursula glanced over at me. "You think he followed her?"

"Maybe?" I shrugged.

"One thing that made my wig pop, and I've been thinking about it since he said it. He said he thought his money problems were over. Why would he say that when he was declaring bankruptcy? He wanted me to know that paying the bills wouldn't be an issue, you know? He was always poor as shit. So that's weird, right?" Permadette looked back and forth between us.

The waitress brought Ursula another glass of tea and looked annoyed about it.

"Thank you," Ursula said sharply as she took it out of her hands.

"Anything else you can think of, Permadette?" I asked, glancing at my phone. We had to sashay our asses out of here, or we would be pushing it getting over the bridge.

"Only that she wasn't looking forward to seeing Pam From Payroll. Not that I blame her. I knew her, and she's ruined. Total pain in the ass." Permadette grinned.

Ursula drank her tea down quickly once again, and I took a sip of my coffee.

"Urs? We need to get back. Permadette, hon, it was a pleasure to meet you, and thank you for telling us what you know. It was very enlightening." I smiled.

"Alright, then, sisters. See you around and if you're ever back up this way, Ursula, let me know. We'd love to have you as a special guest."

Ursula and Permadette took a selfie for her Instagram. She said it would up her value to the other queens, and how could Ursula say no to that.

We held on tight to each other as we slowly walked downhill. By the time we got to the car, both of us were cramping in our calves and dreading standing in heels all night.

My phone buzzed.

"Hey, Cory. You're never gonna..." Cory told me what happened at rehearsal in various tones of shrieking. It wasn't over. "What! We're on our way back now."

"Fuck... What happened?" Ursula looked at me as if she really didn't want to know. I didn't blame her. This case just kept on giving.

"It's not over. There was another attempt. This time at the bar, again."

I made it home faster than I ever had. All I could think about was what Permadette had told us.

Something didn't add up.

Chapter Eighteen

I drove us straight home. We barely had time to find out all the details and grab our drag bags before heading to Rumors to get ready for night two of the pageant.

I opened the front door, my legs cramping from driving and climbing the Golden Hills of San Francisco in a hurry. Cory was pacing around the living room, looking like he had been through it today. Even his hair looked wild.

"Cory, honey!" I walked over and hugged him. He melted into my embrace. "Are you ok? How's Vivienne?"

"It was horrible. We strapped her into her harness, and as we pulled her up and over the curtain, she fell from about five feet in the air. She hit the stage so hard, and we were all just stunned. We secured her in, and... I couldn't understand what happened. Then Vivienne saw her arm. OMG, Vic... I have never heard a scream like that before."

"Broken bones hurt, baby. What did the doctor say? Is she going to be alright?" Ursula chimed in from the couch, where she had put her feet up on the coffee table.

"It was just a fracture, so they set it and gave her a cast. The doctor said she should stay in bed, but Vivienne said there was no way she wasn't competing. She's already got the hot glue gun out and putting sequins on it. She's changed her talent, of course."

"What did Harper say?" I walked over and poured myself a small glass of bourbon. "Urs? You want some?"

"Ooh, girl! Yes, we have time for a little something, something." Ursula said quickly.

"Harper wanted to know where you ran off to. I told him you and Urs were having a girl's day. He didn't buy it, by the way." He finally stopped shuffling around and sat down in the chair across from Ursula. "I have been a hot mess all day. Jesus. That sound as she hit..."

"What did Harper say about the accident? He checked it out, right?" I rolled my eyes and took a quick sip of the warm liquid. I was going to need this tonight.

"Of course. He said the rope had been cut and took it as evidence. But we had our hands and DNA all over that harness. It was just hanging, and when we lifted her, it snapped just as someone had planned."

"He's sure it was cut? Shit. Why her? It's her first

year in the pageant." I snapped. She was my friend, and I was pissed that someone came after her. That made no sense... Unless. "She really did surprise everyone last night. Her outfit for the business attire and her interview outshone the other girls. Is that why?"

"Maybe? Her interview alone made the other girls look like idiots. Maybe she had done too well, and someone didn't want to take any chances with her talent. Who's watched the talent rehearsals, Cory?" Ursula rubbed her feet between sips of bourbon.

"Just my local staff, the bar crew, Joey, and whoever the girls brought with them." He shrugged.

"Has anyone hung back after their queen rehearsed and watched anyone else?"

"No. I have made sure of it." Cory shook his head.

"Someone perceived her as a serious threat and decided she was too much competition. Either that or someone is just out to hurt drag queens. Falling from five feet is scary and could easily hurt you, but you would have to fall just right to be killed. I think that just like the girls that were poisoned and the snake in Judy's bed, these were attempts at stopping them from competing. Not actually trying to kill them." Ursula looked into her bourbon and swirled it as if it were a crystal ball. "So are we back to thinking it's one of the contestants. They would be the only ones to really get something out of it."

"It just doesn't feel right..." I sighed. "And from

everything I learned about the competition world, the sponsors have just as much to either gain or lose. Who else would have access to…"

"But they don't. The only people present at the water poisoning were the contestants. None of the sponsors were in the building after I poured that water." Cory's words were like a gentle slap. I had wanted Domino to be the villain too badly. But Cory was right. My own prejudices against him had led me down the wrong path. What had I missed? "I guess we may not have noticed someone sneaking in. They could have ducked behind the bar, and we may have never seen them."

"So, a contestant?" Ursula sighed. "Girl, we gotta get to the bar so we can beat our mugs."

I downed my cocktail, and we grabbed our bags and headed to the club. I really wanted to call Harper and find out what his investigation had uncovered today. I just didn't have the time right now, and that sucked. I was feeling emotional and could really use his arms around me before I transform into Raven.

Then into Vicki.

Then back into Raven.

Jesus, I was about to have a long night.

We were the first to arrive at Rumors besides the staff. So many of the tables had 'reserved' on them, and I asked for Hank to save a seat for Vicki. She was going to arrive late, as was her prerogative. Ursula and I went into our small dressing room and started getting ready.

I had just finished my underpaint when the girls began to arrive. Their voices drifted into our room from their own. They sounded scared. Another attempt meant they could be next. I didn't blame them. I was scared, too.

"Girl! What the fuck, sis! I heard about your... Look at that cast. You go bitch!" One of the girls, I think it was Shae Black, said loudly. I stood up and glanced over at Ursula, who was putting on some large lashes, and pointed to the dressing room next door. Vivienne must have arrived.

I walked out and stood in the doorway. The girls glanced my way, and Vivienne turned slowly, her right arm in a rainbow sequined cast that sparkled in the light. She puffed her cheeks up and blew out air in a loud exhale. I took a step forward and gingerly took her in my arms.

"You ok, baby?" I whispered.

"That answer is no, momma. I am not, nor will I be ok, until this shit of a pageant is over. My arm should hurt, but I'm so high I barely know my name." She sighed, and I let go and took her left hand in mine. "My talent is going to be off the fucking rails, sis."

"Your cast looks amazing. If you need any help tonight..."

"It's fine, hon. I have someone coming to help me with my makeup and my dress, and well... everything, since I am now not handicapable." She bugged her eyes out. "But I'm going to be fine."

"I'm here, too." Shae stepped up behind her. "I'll make sure she's in show shape, and so will one of my stylists if she needs it. We're all sticking together. It feels safer that way."

"Damn right. You come after one of us. You come after all of us." Karen said passionately.

"Girls... I am so sorry that this is happening. Ursula and I feel completely helpless and... If you see or hear anything that makes you question anything, you let one of us know, ok?" I stared at them, and they nodded.

Looking at them in their show of solidarity made it impossible to think that one of them could be the person doing all of this. It was maddening, but I was starting to believe Ursula was right. They were the only ones who have been here.

"Go finish getting ready. You look like shit." Vivienne touched me gently on the cheek. "You worry about everyone but yourself, hon. Annita Mann will be here in a few minutes, and she'll take good care of me, you know it. She can beat a mug better than anyone."

"Oh, girl. We'll tell you if you're starting to look like Hagatha, baby." Eatta Twinkie laughed.

"Don't worry, girls. If she fucks up, I'll murder her on the spot." Vivienne winked at me.

"Girl, you shouldn't make jokes about murder when we're embroiled in the middle of a murder mystery." Pam From Payroll made the sign of the cross.

"Who's joking," Vivienne said in her best Bette Davis impersonation. It really was fantastic. "I may not be Agatha Christie, but I am a bitch. And a bitch has to *do* what a bitch has to *do*."

The girls all giggled, and I turned around and made my exit back to my own dressing room.

"Did Vivienne just threaten to kill someone?" Ursula laughed huskily. "Child... Bad timing."

Chapter Nineteen

"Hey, you filthy mother fuckers! Who's ready to get this party started tonight!" Ursula yelled into her microphone after the girls did their opening number. The two of us walked between the queens as they held their final pose. Tonight's opening number was about California celebrities. I'll admit, the girls looked fabulous in their impersonation looks.

"Girls... Why are you standing here frozen? Don't you have a pageant to compete in?" I slapped Pussina on the ass. Tonight, she was in her best Beyonce realness, looking authentic and fabulous. She giggled, and they all broke formation and walked off stage to change to their talent looks. "I was starting to think I walked into Bergdorf Goodman's, and the mannequins had come alive, Ursula.

"Honey, I'm just glad someone came as Eartha Kitt.

It was thrrrrrilling." She purred in her best Eartha imitation.

"Tonight, our queens are going to be giving you their most sickening, fishy, body-ody-ody looks as they thrill and excite you in the night; I always love the most, the talent competition. Who's excited to watch these girls death-drop and make you gag over their eleganza?" The crowd screamed and whistled. Maple bay was in rare form today.

"These girls are fierce, Raven. Hopefully, none of them will choke tonight." She turned and looked at me quickly, her large afro whipping around.

"Why, Ursula? Are you afraid of a crying drag queen?"

"Girl... The mascara alone would be a queen-made disaster. We'd have to call in the toxic cleanup crew to handle that mess. No more tears, Raven." She pointed at me.

I pointed back to her. "No more tears."

The music blared over the speakers, and Ursula and I began our number to the diva of all diva's, Ms. Barbra Streisand and Donna Summer. We lip-synced our asses off and somehow remembered the choreography that we hadn't had much of a chance to rehearse. We did have other things on our minds.

In the end, we both started laughing, and I winked at my drag sister. If this pageant hadn't been a murder mystery come to life, this would have been a blast. The audience erupted, and I noticed Harper sitting in his usual spot. I blew him a kiss, and Betty Davis punched him in the arm.

"Are you ready to watch our girls weeerk it hard for you tonight?"

"I can't hear you, Maple Bay?" Ursula held her hand to her ear, and the crowd cheered louder.

"Then let's get this party started. Our first queen is from San Diego. Ladies and laddies who want to be ladies, welcome the lovely and most likely to leave a waiter a five percent tip, Pam From Payroll."

Pam and her dancers took the stage, and her number began. She had chosen to lip-sync to a medley of office songs. It was cute, and her choreography was excellent. She really did bring it, and I could see why she was one of the top queens in the competition. The crowd roared for her, especially when nine to five came on. Everyone loves Dolly.

The girls did their talent. Shae Black sang an original dance song that was fifty percent comedy and fifty percent a disco anthem. Her dancers almost fell off the stage at one point, and she looked like she wanted to throttle them. It really wasn't her time, even if she could sing like a diva. But it would be one day. She was as fishy as they came and could walk into a Tennessee Wal-Mart in midday, and no one would bat an eye.

Vivienne, who did so great last night, came out in a brand new opening that didn't require her to break her other arm. Her impressions were fabulous, but because of the drugs she was currently on for pain, her timing was off. Whoever sabotaged her act earlier today had been successful. She was out of the running.

Judy Ghouland was next, and her number was magical if not downright gross. In her trademark zombified Judy Garland makeup, she and her dancers did a bizarre and original version of Get Happy. Once again, parts of her body fell off during the number. By the end, her face was almost skeletal, and by the magic of show business, her dancers ripped off her right arm and started eating it. The audience gasped and then applauded louder for her than anyone else. She could take the whole competition if she had another amazing night tomorrow night.

Ursula and I did our other number. Lady Gaga's Paparazzi, and we made it fun. Ursula peppered little tidbits about celebrity and reality television in between verses, and then the song would start again until she stopped it to tell us more gossip. It really was the high-light of the night because hearing about her brushes with actors and singers, and other reality stars was hilarious.

"Ready for Act Two of our talent competition?" I asked the audience.

"I am. You know Raven... After all that gossip, I really could use a pizza, girl." Raven lowered her voice and looked at me seriously, her hand on her hip. "My sugar's low, baby. Would you go get me a cheese pizza? I'll take over for a bit if you just scoot on over to Domenico's and bring it to me."

"A pizza? Is this some kind of stunt, Ursula?" I mocked surprise. In truth, the pizza had already been called in and would be delivered to the back door in thirty minutes. Ursula gave them a big tip to be exactly on time. Hopefully, they would be—our plan, as stupid and juvenile as it was, depended on it.

"No, girl. I am seriously hungry. You know it takes a lot of pizza to keep my girlish figure." She looked out at the audience and mugged stupidly at them. They ate it up. After her celebrity confessions, she could do whatever she wanted.

"A cheese pizza? Ok, girl. I'll do it."

"Let's hear it for Raven, everyone. Next time we see her, she's gonna share a pizza with me up on his stage. If you haven't seen two ravenous drag queens' scarf down a pizza like a velociraptor, you should consider yourself blessed, but tonight... Oh, tonight... you are gonna witness such an event. Grease everywhere, baby! This stage is gonna get so slick, queens are gonna think it's an ice skating rink."

I walked off stage and out the door just as we had planned. I ran around to the back of the bar and entered into the small breezeway we created for the queens to come and go and ran into my dressing room. I wiped off the garish eyeshadow I wore and replaced it quickly with a natural lid. Valerie Rage was living onstage, according to the crowd. I knew she would be exciting to watch. I changed my lipstick color and slathered more base to cover the rouge on my cheeks, which I then repainted. I looked like Raven Ravonne had morphed into Vicki. I changed wigs quickly and threw on a scarf and a new dress. I pinned the large brimmed hat in place so it would provide shade to my face and threw on a pair of eyeglasses that I sometimes wore as Vicki. They had a tint to them, thankfully, and that would help hide my eyes from view. This was Vicki Dean's incognito realness, and I was living for it.

I ran back around the bar and had to catch my breath by the time I got to the front door. Crap, I was out of shape.

Dammit Janet was already onstage, and the audience was enjoying her. I sneaked in and sat down at the table I had reserved, and Henry noticed me and brought me my drink as we had asked him to.

"Here you go, Ms. Dean." He whispered. "This is from Victor and Ursula." I nodded my appreciation.

Janet was quite good. It wasn't amazing, but she could actually dance her ass off and was quite surprising with her ability to flip and cartwheel in giant heels. The crowd loved her, but it wasn't anything that you couldn't see in your local drag bar. She ended in the splits, and the crowd cheered for her.

Ursula sashayed back onto the stage and pulled out her phone. She mimed punching in a number and waited a few seconds. She rolled her eyes at the audience.

"Just like a queen... She probably got her phone on silent or some shit. Oh! Raven? Bitch, where's my mother fucking pizza? Mmm-hmm... Tell him to bake it faster. Ok... Fine, girl." She used her finger to hang up the phone and looked out at the audience. "Never send a queen to do the job of a college boy. Apparently, she's decided to have a beer while she's waiting. This is your girl. She belongs to all of you, Maple Bay, and I know you loooove her. Especially, him." She pointed to Harper, who had no idea what was happening.

"But while we are waiting for the next girl's set to be put in place, let's have a special guest, shall we? This wasn't planned, and she might slap me, but give her a big hand anyway. Vicki Dean, girl! Get on up here." She yelled to me, and I sighed dramatically, the audience turning to see if I was really here. I waved and carried my purse up to the stage as well as my cocktail. You couldn't be too careful around here, apparently.

"Vicki Dean. Do you know how excited I was to meet you, girl?" Ursula pursed her lips and jumped up and down like a schoolgirl. "Best selling mystery author and the sleuth in stilettos, herself."

"Well, Ursula, I can't wear a heel as high as you girls do. I would topple over. I prefer a sensible heel so I can run away if I need to." The audience laughed. "You never know when you need to make an escape."

I glanced down, and Harper looked like he had seen a ghost. Betty Davis had grabbed his arm and was chatting his ear off. She was shocked I showed up, but maybe now she would leave me alone.

"So, tell us about your next book. Cory, your

adorable assistant, was telling me it comes out later this year."

"Yeah, that's what they tell me." I giggled. "Of course, it's not finished yet. Why am I here instead of working? Don't tell my agent."

"What's the new book called? You know us fans all want to know."

"The title hasn't been released yet, actually. But you can order the Untitled New Release by Vicki Dean at any bookseller if you want to pre-order," I mugged, and the audience ate it up.

"Come on, Vicki... Just a little hint."

"Well, Ursula...Just between us girls and most of the town of Maple Bay? Well, and Betty Davis is here, so it'll be all over the radio tomorrow. That's ok, I guess. You want a scoop?" I asked the crowd and Ursula nodded exaggeratedly, her afro flopping back and forth. She had great timing. No wonder she became a star.

"Fine... It's called Murder of Convenience, and it's already on the New York Times Bestselling list. I'm still writing it, Ursula." I shrugged. "Maybe I should make you a character in the book?"

"Would you do that? You have no idea how much that would mean to me, Vicki. I'm not the murderer, am I?" She turned quickly to me and grabbed my arm. "Vicki, don't make me the murderer, please."

"I promise, darling. I could never do that to a great diva such as yourself. We girls have to stick together." I winked. "Now, don't you have a show to finish or something?"

"I do. This has been one of the best nights of my life." Ursula kissed me on the cheek.

"Just don't add me to your tales of celebrity gossip. Remember, I could kill you in my next book."

"Ladies and Laddies who want to be ladies, Ms. Vicki Dean."

I walked off stage and waved at Betty and Harper as I made my way back to the table. Ursula announced the next contestant, Eatta Twinkie, and I snuck out the back door and met the delivery boy who was right on time. I then hightailed it back through the breezeway and into my dressing room. Jesus, the pizza smelled good.

I have no idea what Eatta was doing out there, but the crowd was clapping and applauding throughout her number. By the time she was finished, I had thrown on a ton of makeup, doing my best to quickly paint my face as I had done before, then I smeared Vaseline over it, making my skin look as greasy as possible. I opened the pizza box and laid the pizza on the napkins I placed, putting only one slice back in the box.

I then ran in my Raven heels, which were much higher than Vicki's, through the back door. I stopped quickly and pressed myself up against the wall, making sure the door didn't slam behind me.

I wasn't alone.

"I really don't give a damn." A high nasal voice hissed. "I am over you're shit. These positions should be fixed, and you know it. You don't want me to make a phone call, do you?"

Another voice whispered, and I could barely hear him. It sounded like he said, doing... can... maybe. I tried to glance around the corner but could only see two long shadows.

"You better. Things get bad for you if you don't. Remember, I know things about you." The back door slammed shut, and there was no only one shadow standing there.

"Shit!" Whoever it was hissed. He followed the other person inside.

I ran around the building, wishing I knew who was outside arguing. All of this happened in the time Eatta performed her number and Karen had begun hers. I was breathing so hard, and my heart was racing so fast, I was honestly afraid I might pass out. I waited by the front door and watched Karen, who was up onstage living in her moment.

It was pretty damn fantastic. She had mixed together a compilation of when Karen's attack footage, and she accosted the audience with her lip-sync, which was totally on point. She had mixed it with Meredith Brook's Bitch, and it was hilarious. The audience was laughing their asses off and really into it. Damn, she was excellent.

When she finished. Ursula walked out on stage.

"Have you seen a drag queen delivery girl with a pizza? What the hell is taking her so…"

"I'm here!" I burped loudly as I walked towards the stage, staggering a little as if I were drunk. "I had a cocktail while I waited… Or two." I said loudly to one of the audience members as I used their shirt as a napkin. "Sorry… I'm a little greasy."

"Raven Ravonne! You didn't." She stared me down and tapped her foot loudly on the stage.

"Just a little. I got hungry walking all the way over there."

"Girl! It's across the street."

"In these heels? That's like ten blocks." I handed her the box.

"Child, this feels light as hell." Raven opened it and showed the open box to the audience. They all ooohed at me.

"One piece! What's on your face?"

"Nothing… I washed it." I said stupidly. We were spit-balling this, and I was coming up blank. Thankfully Ursula took the lead.

"Mmm-Hmm… Looks like pizza grease. What do you all think, Maple Bay?" They all agreed loudly. Harper especially.

Ursula took out the last slice of pizza and dropped the box on the stage. She took a big bite and waved at the audience. "Good night Maple Bay and we will see you tomorrow when we crown a new Ms. Cali West Coast. Tomorrow night is swimwear and evening gown. Be here or be queer. Bitch, you ate all the pizza!"

She chased me offstage, and we fell into a fit of laughter as soon as we made it to the dressing room.

Vivienne poked her head in. "You two are weird."

Ursula almost choked on her pizza.

All I could think about was that conversation I overheard. Who was that?

Chapter Twenty

"**R**eally, Eatta, was that good?" I asked, surprised. "I could hear the audience going crazy, but... I guess I'm just a little shocked."

"After that, she is the one to beat, I would think." Cory agreed. "I mean, it all depends on the judges and how well she does tomorrow night. But if she finishes as strong as her talent, no one will remember her gaffes the first night."

"Yeah... That interview was bad. Like train wreck bad." I laughed. All of the girls had gone home, and we were sitting around the bar, thankfully out of drag, having a drink and trying to relax a little. "Joey! Get off your computer and come join us."

"Yes, Joey." Cory rolled his eyes. I thought they might be on their way to having a little thing, but apparently, there was trouble in paradise.

"Sorry. Sending an email. I've already gotten two complaints about the random order of the contestants for their talent. One thinks their girl shouldn't have followed another. One thinks his girl was being set up for failure. I swear you cannot please these people." Joey let loose in a tirade he had been holding inside too long.

"Girl, let it out. All that anger causes cancer." Ursula said seriously. "What are you drinking, Joey?"

"I'm drinking vodka-seven, Urs." He shut his laptop and sat down beside Ursula. Interesting that he didn't sit by Cory. I glanced over at my sweet himbo, and he seemed completely unfazed. Maybe I had imagined the chemistry between them.

"Henry, honey. Give this man a double." Ursula cooed.

"Did you decide about the tribute video, Joey? Will it be at the beginning tomorrow night or before the crowning?" Cory asked, leaning onto the bar to look around us.

"Maybe the beginning. I feel like it would be weird to do it before we crown the new queen. We already have last year's winner coming in for her swan song, and that's been a shit show, too. Why do I do this..." He shook his head disgustedly.

"Because you love drag, honey. You love the art form and everything it does for our community. You have championed all the girls and shined a spotlight on what we do and why it's important hon. You do

Jesus' work, baby." Ursula put her arm around him. "We've known each other for a while. Maybe not that well, but I see you. I know how hard you work."

Joey looked like someone had just punched him in the face instead of trying to make him feel better. "That... Thank you, Urs. It's not as true as I would like. Sometimes... When I first started, yes. But the joy of it has been taken away from me. I think I have to step down for my own good if they let me."

"Lord. You sound like you are being held at gunpoint, hon. Cheer up. This year is almost over."

"It's been a hell of a way to end it, that's for sure. I had no idea it would be like this, or I wouldn't have... I guess, even done it. I think that's why I should get out... if I can. I wanted to last year, but... They like me where I am."

We had nothing more to say. Damn, Joey was depressing as shit, and we were already in mourning. Henry blasting Lana Del Rey and The Indigo Girls wasn't helping.

"I wonder how Lil' Debbie would have done if given a chance? She was pretty damn talented. I think she would have torn up talent and interview but then came out here in a shitty evening gown. Her taste was... not exceptional. She always had those gowns she got on consignment." Ursula patted Joey on the back. "You knew her better than me, though. She'd been doing pageants for a long time."

"Yeah. She deserved better. That's... I mean, who

would expect that. It's just horrible, and when you can't do a damn thing about it... I hate it! I wish she was here yelling at me instead of us talking about a tribute video." Joey teared up. "They all treated her like shit - the other queens and the sponsors, except for Heather, of course. She loved her. I think she was the only one who actually understood her. But Lil' Debbie didn't make it easy on anyone. She always had to get in the last word."

"I guess she still got it, in the end, huh? We'll be talking about her for the next decade." Cory nodded.

"She just couldn't keep her nose out of anything. Of course, this happened. She grabbed onto any opportunity."

Ursula glanced over at me.

"That's pointed. What couldn't she keep her nose out of, Joey?" I reached over and patted him on the back. He was unraveling. Tears started flowing down his face, and he swallowed a sob. He held his hand up and scrunched up his face trying to regain control of his emotions. It took a second.

"I'm sorry..."

"It's ok, hon. So Lil' Debbie was in some kind of trouble?" Ursula continued, rubbing small circles on his back.

"What? No... Not that I... Just when things went bad with Carson, she was flailing blindly. She was going to sign with Domino, and he's... I mean, he's seedy, but aren't they all? Carson is just as bad as all the others and don't even get me started on Harry. Why are all these bar owners so... bad? You have it good here. I'm just sorry that all of this was dumped here on your town. I wish I had known." He wiped his eyes and took a deep breath.

"Were Carson and Barry... dating?" I asked quietly, dropping my voice to a murmur. That was not what I was expecting, but it closed a hole in the investigation.

"Yeah, for a short time, I think. Honestly, I'm not really sure. It just seemed like they... you know... That's all." He ran his fingers through his hair and sat up straight. "Sorry, I shouldn't be speaking about things I don't really know. I hate gossip because it always makes things go bad."

Ursula stared at him and nodded slowly.

We said our goodbyes and grabbed our drag bags. Joey said he was gonna head back to his hotel. His phone wouldn't stop buzzing. Someone was trying really hard to get a hold of him and complain about something.

We got in the car, and Ursula turned to look at me. Cory popped his head forward to be a part of the conversation.

"Last night, Vivienne pulled ahead of all the other girls. Then she was attacked. Tonight, Eatta Twinkie showed them all up by a mile. If there's a pattern here, it would make sense that someone might try to stop her from finishing the pageant, doesn't it? If not her, then maybe Karen or Judy, again. They both had strong showings and did well on the first night."

"Well, it's something, at least. I'll call Harper and have him join us. I still can't get what Joey said out of my head. Carson and Barry? Carson lied to us if that's true."

"Oh, girl! You know, I have a friend in San Diego, and I completely forgot about that ho. She won this pageant a few years ago and walked away from drag shortly after. She owns a bar down there, now. She might have a little info. I'll call her when we get home, and you talk to Harper. Two birds, one convo, honey." Ursula stuck her tongue in the corner of her cheek, and I pulled out onto the main road to my house.

"You said something that surprised me when you were talking to Joey about Barry. You said she had crappy taste and second-hand gowns?"

"Oh, yeah. She always does well in the pageants, but evening wear and business attire kill her every time. Oh sorry. She just couldn't compete against the other girls in those categories. Heather is fine as a sponsor, but her bar can't afford the kind of outfits that the other sponsors can. Why?" Ursula glanced back over to me.

"When I was in her room the day she... you know... I saw her gowns. They were insanely beautiful and looked like they were incredibly expensive. Maybe that's why she was going to declare bankruptcy? She spent all her money on this pageant?" I shrugged, trying to get it to make sense in my head. It was right there and driving me insane.

"Maybe? But if she spent that kind of money and then had over four grand to give Permadette... That's a lot of money, ho." Ursula bit her bottom lip. "She did say she came into a windfall of some kind. I just wish we knew what it was." We thought about it all the way home.

Harper was waiting in the living room watching one of our favorite HGTV couples as they argued about tearing down a wall. At least, that's probably what they were arguing about. With them, it could be anything. You could tell that they loathed each other.

"Can we chat for a second?" I grabbed him by the hand and led him into the kitchen. Cory took his place on my sofa.

"I didn't know Vicki was making an appearance tonight. Seems like a lot of work for Betty Davis." He chuckled. "This has been... Nothing that helps us came back on the rope being cut. It looks like it was done by a razor blade. There was no one on the outside cameras, so it had to be done sometime during the day. That's all we can figure out." He leaned on my small island, and the look on his face told me how he was feeling. He wanted justice for the victims, but the leads were thin or non-existent. He was frustrated and knew the pageant was coming to an end.

"Ursula had an idea, and I think it's the best one we have," I told him about how Vivienne may have been targeted for outshining one of the other girls. How we were concerned about Eatta, Judy, and Karen. He nodded and picked up his phone.

"Jensen, can you grab a couple of the guys and set up surveillance at the two hotels tonight? Yeah... We want to... Do you have a list of who's in each room?" He turned to me and realized the answer. "Cory! Do you know which rooms the girls are in?"

Cory walked in with his folder and looked through it. "Eatta is at the Beach View, and the other two are at Maple Bay. Here are their room numbers." He slid the folder over to Harper, who gave Jensen the room numbers.

"Hey, get as close as you can and keep someone outside at each place in plain clothes. If the killer tries to strike tonight, we want to be ready."

Ursula bounded down the stairs, her heels making loud clomps as she made her way to us.

"You are not going to believe this." She shook her head dramatically, her eyes wide with newfound knowledge.

Yeah.

She was right.

But now, some of the pieces were starting to fall in place. I thought I knew who the killer was.

Chapter Twenty-One

*G*od... Stakeouts are boring.

I mean, Harper and I could be cuddling on the bed, but instead, he is sitting at the small table with his headphones on. He was able to put two surveillance bugs outside Eatta's door without anyone noticing, as far as we could tell. It was just us in the hotel room, and there was nothing funny happening if you get my drift.

I yawned. He had hung some contraption onto the wall that had a built-in microphone directed into Eatta's room, which was right next door. It was late, but according to Harper, she hadn't been off the phone since we got here. He listened to her blow-by-blow retelling of the pageant tonight as she was watching Little House on the Prairie. That alone was surprising.

Ursula was with Letitia as they watched Karen's

room, and Cory and Jensen kept a watchful eye on Judy's. Every now and then, the officers would radio Harper and tell him that all was calm. It was almost midnight.

Jesus, I was bored and sleepy.

Maybe we were wrong.

"Vic? How accurate do you think this intel was from Ursula's friend? I mean, I woke up the judge to get these warrants, and he was not very happy, even if he did understand the necessity. I'm just... I feel on edge." He stuck out his bottom lip in the most adorable pout. I really wanted to stand up and go put my arms around him, but I was too damn beat. It had been a hell of a day, and my feet were killing me.

"Ursula believes it, so I guess I do too. This isn't her first time involved in a police investigation, you know."

"Yeah, I know her husband's a detective. But this is not the direction I thought this was going to go."

"Hey, at least it's something. I just can't believe we couldn't turn anything up in our background search. But the bar scene is... well, sometimes shady. This is the kind of gossip that would have helped us if we had been in the same city. We would have found it then. But, no one here was privy to it, except for..."

"She hung up the phone. God, I literally can't believe the other person even spoke. She just rattled on and on... She's very excited about doing so well tonight, though." Harper looked over at me with his tired eyes.

"I just wished we could have... I mean, this information would have changed everything, wouldn't it? At least, we could have focused more on it when we did the interviews." I curled into a ball on the bed and fluffed the pillow under my head.

"You're tired, babe. Try to get some sleep, and if I hear anything, I'll wake you up." He said softly, a small smile turning up the corners of his mouth.

"No. That's not fair. I've gotten more sleep than you. I hear you getting up and going downstairs to look over everything again." I fought to keep my eyes open. Shit, lying down was a bad idea.

"I hate not being able to follow the crumbs. But there just weren't many. It's frustrating." He sighed and sat back in his chair. "If this is all true, we got very lucky."

"I know. All you can do is your best, babe, and you always do. I couldn't see it either. How would we know that this all came down to money? I just can't believe it was..."

"Yep. That was a surprise, but it also makes sense with everything else you told me about Lil'... Barry's windfall of cash. The two have to be linked. How he kept his nose so clean with the authorities is what surprises me. If this is what we think... It's going to open up a much larger investigation there."

"It makes sense. I know it does."

But nothing happened. The digital clock in the room kept changing, and after a few hours, I did close my eyes. I knew nothing until I felt Harper gently shake me awake.

I glanced over at the clock. Six in the morning... Shit.

Harper held a finger to his lips. Something was happening.

"She's up and sounds like she's getting ready. I hear drawers opening and her grumbling. Oh, she's unlatching her door."

I ran to the window and peered carefully out of the side of the drapes. Eatta was wearing running shorts and a t-shirt. It looked like she was about to go jogging or exercising. I saw her walk past the unmarked patrol car.

"Danny. You see her?" Harper said into his radio.

"Want me to follow her?" he answered tiredly.

"Yeah. Let's hope she's not a good jogger. Keep your eyes open." Harper sighed.

"I really thought we would have something happen. But... Nothing did happen to the girls while they were there, did it? Only Barry had a visitor. All the others were more... sneaky. Harper?" I leaned against the front door, my mouth agape.

"What, babe?" He stood up and came over to me, and took me in his arms.

"It's two different people. They might be connected, but the person doing these other things is not the same person who killed Barry... Holy shit." I knew. There was only one person it could be. Only one other person besides Cory could have poisoned the water, and we... How blind was I? Why didn't I ever think of him as a suspect before?

Harper held up his hand. He heard something.

"Vic? Someone is inside Eatta's room. I think. I heard something."

"Is it the TV?"

He shook his head no. I glanced over at our bathroom, which was set at the back of the room, and noticed a window. I pointed to it and dashed over. I carefully peered out, and sure enough, a pair of shoes floated in the air. They weren't Nikes.

I ran to the door and opened it. Harper hot on my heels, and he used the master key as quietly as possible to unlock Eatta's door. It clicked, and he threw it open, his gun drawn, and I had never been more turned on in my life.

There stood Joey in a pair of sweats, a boxcutter in his hand with the razor point out. He wore a look of shock and immediately burst into tears.

"Drop the razor," Harper ordered, and he did. "Kick it over here."

Joey tried to kick it and only succeeded in pushing it a few inches. His second try pushed it closer to us. I grabbed one of Eatta's t-shirts that were lying on the floor and carefully picked it up. I would bet that this was the tool that was used to cut Vivienne's ropes. I wrapped the razor with the t-shirt and pulled down the sharp edge back into the casing.

"I'm... I'm sorry. I didn't... I..."

"You are under arrest." Harper walked over to him and read him his rights as he handcuffed him.

"I wasn't going to hurt her... I was just going to rip up her gowns, so she... she..." Joey hung his head and started crying harder.

"Joey?" I asked, bending down to get on his eye level from his kneeling position. Something he had said last night now made sense. He was one of the shadows I heard talking last night, too. I would bet on it. "Did someone make you do this?"

He nodded shamefully.

I bent down and whispered in his ear, and he nodded again.

"Why was he blackmailing you?" I said compassionately.

"I got into trouble financially and started... I used some of the pageant money. He was on our board at the time, and he found some expenses that he questioned. It was a lot over a few years, and he's been holding it against me for the last two years. This year he wanted me to... make sure the other girls didn't get in the way, you know. He wanted an easy win."

"Did you murder Barry, Joey?" Harper asked after radioing the others.

"God, no! Of course, I didn't. I would never do that,

but who knows what he would ask of me next. I'm... I'm just glad it's over. I'm sorry, Victor. So fucking sorry."

"So, you poisoned the water after you got your own glass?"

He nodded. "I made sure to put in just enough to make them sick. It wouldn't have killed them." He said quickly, tears falling onto the gross beige carpet. "I swear! And I made sure the snake was not venomous, and I didn't know that Vivienne would fall from that high up. I thought it would rip right away. I... I didn't want to hurt anyone. But I did. These are my girls and I... I'm so sorry."

I heard movement from outside, and Eatta stood there standing at the door with a shocked look on her face.

"What the hell's happening."

"I'll explain it later, hon. It's ok. Please, keep this to yourself. No gossip. I mean it." I said sternly, and she nodded. "This is life or death."

Harper led Joey out of the room and down to the unmarked car. He handed over his phone and offered the code. Now that he was caught, he was prepared to tell us all he knew. However, I didn't think he knew anything about Barry's murder. The two crimes were connected in a way, but not really.

He didn't know the identity of the killer, and he should have if he had thought about it hard enough.

Of course, he was too concerned with saving his own ass and doing the bidding of a crook who was desperate enough to do anything to win.

I knew who the killer was, and it was time to make him pay.

Chapter Twenty-Two

I went home and laid down for a minute to collect my thoughts. I was too wired to even try to take a nap. Ursula and Cory had passed out on the couch, and I knew I had to work fast if I wanted to finish this before the last night of the pageant. We didn't have enough on him yet. With what Joey confessed, we had him on blackmail and intent to cause harm and terror, but he could still walk on murdering Lil' Debbie. It was all hearsay and gossip, and I was sure he had been careful in his shady business dealings, or he would have been on the radar of the authorities.

Harper was not happy when I told him he couldn't bring him in yet. But he knew I was right.

I needed to find a way to take him down, to get him to admit what he did. It had to be him. There were now too many connections I had finally put together for it to be anyone else. But how could I get him to tell me the truth?

I had to take a chance. If it blew up in my face, then that's what would happen. But if it didn't. Lil' Debbie… Barry could finally get the justice he deserved. We all owed him that. He was our sister.

I took a long shower and let the warm water revive me enough to get me through this day. Tonight would be its own problem. A gallon of coffee would keep me going to the end. I just had to make it there.

I slowly painted my face to assume Vicki's identity. Her cheekbones and nose, her mouth and brow took over my features as I slowly painted my face. It was time for her to take over for a while. Her words and particular way of thinking were who I needed right now.

I stared at myself as I slowly stood up and let her inside. Her posture and mannerisms slowly took over, and I shed Victor as Vicki slid down over me. I walked to the closet and chose a black pinstripe suit. The skirt was short enough to give me the freedom to run if it came to that. A light grey blouse underneath the suit completed the look. I wore black boots with a very small chunky heel, and I zipped them up over my calves.

Vicki's hair was starting to look like she had been caught in a windstorm. I had taken it off and on so much without the time to properly care for it. I brushed it before placing it on my head and carefully pulled my bangs through the lace front to hide any lines. I teased my hair and sprayed it into place before pinning it tightly to my head. I gave my head a good shake to make sure it was firmly on before walking out the door.

I sent the text and shook Cory awake.

"Is it time?" he asked breathlessly as he woke up in a fright.

"Shit... What time is it?" Ursula asked as she stretched her arms above her head. "Damn... Momma's got dragon breath. Do I have time to brush?"

"It's time to circle the wagons. You know what you have to do." I sat down on the arm of the chair and tried to stop my hand from shaking. Yes, I was scared. I would be a fool not to be.

"Alright, momma. We got you." Ursula placed her hand in Cory's and squeezed it, giving him strength. He had been shocked by Joey's actions and blamed himself for not seeing it.

I had two hours, and there was something I still needed to do before this mystery played out its final act.

⚜

J pulled into the back of the bar and noticed that the parking lot was empty. I was alone, and Rumors wouldn't open until later this afternoon. Cory made sure that Henry wouldn't arrive early to get set up for the day. The bar was mine, and I used my key to unlock the back door, leaving it cracked so the killer would have easy access.

I walked into the dark bar quietly and grabbed a chair from the front row, and set it down in the middle of the stage. I turned on one stage light that would shine behind me, illuminating me enough but not blurring my vision. I had adjusted to the dark. I sat and waited, crossing my ankles gingerly underneath me. My hands folded in my lap as I took deep breaths.

It wouldn't be long. I told him when to meet me, even if he didn't know it was me that he would be seeing. God... My heart was beating out of my chest. Why did I put myself in these types of positions? Hadn't I learned my lesson the last time one of my plans went awry and I almost died?

I looked at my watch.

Shit. Had I been here that long already?

He was late. Maybe he wasn't coming. Maybe he realized that something was wrong and had decided to run.

The back door banging loudly made me flinch. Was it him?

"Joey?" His high nasal voice asked from the back. His shoes clipped slowly on the concrete as he made his way towards the main bar. "You here?"

I cleared my throat and heard his footsteps getting closer as he made his way through the narrow hallway. He paused in the doorway, just a shadow to my eyes.

"Hey. Have you seen Joey?" he asked, his voice tight and unsure.

"Come in, Mr. DeVoor. I think you and I need to have a chat. Joey's not here." I snipped coldly.

"He sent me a text message." He took a few steps into the room.

"Yes. That wasn't Joey. You know, sending a text from someone else's number isn't that difficult if you know how, and I do. I thought you might respond to Joey since he is in charge of the pageant." I didn't want to overplay my hand. If he knew that Joey had been arrested, he might decide to end this conversation. I had to keep him hooked and feeling like he had the upper hand.

"Why would you do such a thing?" Another step towards me.

"I thought I would see if my suspicions were true. Do you mind if I call you Carson?"

"Whatever floats your boat. Why did you want to see me?" He almost hissed. He sensed that he wasn't going to like this conversation.

"Well, I hate to accuse someone of murder before giving them a chance to explain why I'm wrong. That would not be good PR for a mystery writer, would it?"

"Murder?" He laughed. "You think that I... That's pretty fucking hilarious, you know that. What? You're a comedian, Vicki? You got balls, I'll give you that."

"Ms. Dean, please," I answered dryly. "I think I have put all the pieces together, Carson, and I'm afraid that it all points to you. You're not half as clever as you thought. There's always a trail, and it leads directly to you."

"Lady, you're batshit crazy, you know that? I could sue you for defamation." He took another few steps towards me, pointing his finger as menacingly as he could. I admit it was quite intimidating.

I laughed. "Oh, Carson. Do you really think I would ask for this meeting if I didn't already have the goods? I just need to deliver them to our dear sheriff's hands, and your goose, as they say, is cooked. Would you like to know what I know?"

"You need to deliver them... Ok, Ms. Dean," he said snidely. "Let's hear it. What do you have on me."

"I know that you were blackmailing Joey. I found a number of communications to him where you outright say it. Carson..." I tutted. "Really, never put that kind of thing in an email or text. It never goes away. Have you learned anything about the internet? I also know that you were forcing him to scare the girls that are here competing in the hopes to give your own... girl... Pam, I believe, a leg up on the competition. That didn't work out so well, I see. Joey must not have been a very good co-conspirator. He didn't really have the stomach for it, did he?"

He slowly licked his lips. "You have emails and text messages. You said yourself that anyone can hack into those kinds of things and send something as me. It proves nothing."

I laughed again. "No, you fool. It's attached to an IP address, and I'm afraid I had it traced, and it belongs to you. That's hard evidence that will put you away for a good ten to twenty years in the clink, Carson. But it's not the cherry on top. That was Barry, wasn't it?"

"I told you that I..."

"I know. You had no reason to kill him. But you did, didn't you? About twenty thousand dollars worth of reasons, I think."

Carson's eyes widened, and he balled his hands into a fist. I had him. He took another step towards me. I stood up and clasped my hands in front of me.

"That's far enough," I said sternly. "You and Barry started dating, and you promised him the moon to move to San Diego and let you be his sponsor. However, while he was staying with you, he found out a few things about you that he didn't like. You see, dear Lil' Debbie actually confessed to someone, and I found that person, Carson. It took some digging, but this is what I do. I found her, and she led me to another person who confirmed it all to me."

"Sure, I offered Barry a position at my bar, and I would be his sponsor. So what?"

"He discovered your stash, didn't he? You launder money, Carson, and apparently you're quite good at it, because the authorities knew nothing about you. But Barry found it. He found it all, and when he confronted you about it, you hit him and got into a big fight about it. But when he left, he took some of the money with him, didn't he? He stole from you and then took Domino's offer to work for him and move to San Francisco. He had the goods on you. How much more did he ask for besides the thousands he already took?"

"You have nothing!" He shouted and slapped his hand down on the table before taking another step in my direction. I moved behind the chair, placing it between us.

"I have it all." I held up a folder I had placed on the chair seat. He didn't need to know it was empty. "Witness statements and everything, Carson. Barry left a trail of cash that didn't belong to him all the way here. How much more did he want?"

"He was getting nothing!" Carson headed towards me and stopped at the edge of the stage. "I told him so, and he started screaming what he would do if I didn't! How we would ruin me! So I..."

"Killed him?" I asked harshly, spitting the words at him.

"Yes. He was trash and always would be. I tried to help him, but the bitch wouldn't listen, and so I had to stop him from..."

"Doing to you what you did to Joey?"

"Lady... You should have gone to the sheriff first." He stepped up on the stage.

"I did." I smiled, and he knew he was in trouble. He had played right into my hands and believed the stupidest lie of all.

The lights turned on in the bar, and Jensen and

Carpenter stepped out of the shadows. He looked around and lunged for me. Ursula's fist flew out from behind the curtain and connected to his jaw with a loud thud, and he went down.

"You better stay down too, mother fucker." She warned.

Harper stepped out from the back of the stage, his gun drawn, and Jensen and Carpenter ran to the stage and handcuffed him.

"Did you get all of that?" I asked, smiling at him.

"Yes, ma'am, we did." Jensen nodded. "All recorded for posterity, and it sounded to me like he just confessed to murder."

Harper walked over to me and whispered in my ear. "I love you. Are you ok?"

I nodded.

"I think it's only fair, Carson, that you say hello to the ladies you put in harm's way. Girls."

The queens, all in boy drag except for Karen, walked out to the back of the stage. Pam From Payroll looked dazed and distraught. She had been his victim, too. They stared at him as Jensen pulled him to his feet, looking like they all wanted to give him a dose of drag queen justice, and trust me, I'm sure he would rather go to prison than be faced with that.

Harper read Carson his rights, and they took him away. I turned to look at all the queens holding hands and comforting Pam, who had started crying on Judy's shoulder. They all touched her and patted her as they tried to comfort her.

"Girl, you better pull yourself together and try to kick my ass on stage tonight. You are one fierce bitch, you hear me?" Eatta said firmly to Pam, who nodded. Jesus, Pam could ugly cry right up there with Oprah.

"Ursula? I'm going to leave these ladies in your care." I said before turning away and walking slowly out the back door.

I got in my car and started sobbing over the steering wheel.

Why did I do this to myself?

Chapter Twenty-Three

The girls were on fire tonight.

When we first arrived at the bar to start getting ready, they were laughing and helping each other like they had been working together for years. Murder brought them closer, but betrayal made them sisters.

Pam was quieter than normal. Discovering your sponsor and boss had stabbed someone in the head with a stiletto was a sobering experience. The bar would probably close, and she would be forced to find a new home and a new sponsor if she continued in the pageant system. I wouldn't if I were her. This was a stain that she would find hard to erase. But show business did love a comeback.

Earlier, Ursula and I fell asleep on my bed with Cory between us. I don't know how we were able to quiet our troubled minds, but sleep did come, and trust me... We needed that power nap. Even after, I had enough luggage under my eyes that my car wanted baggage fees. Harper woke us up with a phone call telling me that he would be at the bar in time for the show.

The press had gotten wind of the killer being apprehended, and he was busy. After hearing his confession played back to him, Carson asked for his lawyer. He was sitting in a cell waiting for an attorney that didn't have his best interests at heart. Whoever he was laundering money for would be put on the radar, and if he was released on bail, which in this town was not likely, he wouldn't survive long. Those kinds of guys didn't leave loose ends. His best hope was to turn state's evidence as Harper had reminded him.

Only time would tell.

"Girls." I knocked on their door and glanced around at their costumes for this, the last opening number they would ever do together. "I just wanted to say how proud I am of all of you. The pageant has sent a new representative that will be taking over until they find a permanent replacement. I think you know her."

"Hello ladies," Ursula strode into the room, her contralto a purr as she spun in front of them. "I'm only taking the position for a short time, but for now, I am in charge of this bitch, so let's turn it out, shall we?"

They all congratulated her, and Pam smiled wider than all of them. I felt bad for her. She was just another victim in this mystery, and I wished I could make it better for her. She wasn't as bad as she first appeared. I mean, she was still a snotty ho, but facts were facts.

The show began, and the girls lip-synced to songs from the movies. They bounded out on stage as if they owned it and belonged there. I had never seen them be so together and so in sync. Their energy lit the place up, and the crowd responded with thunderous applause.

We followed it up with each of the girls lighting a candle and showing the film tribute to Lil' Debbie. Each of the girls stepped up to the mic and said something sweet about her, even if they didn't know her well. She was one of them, now and forever. The missing piece of a jigsaw puzzle that almost never got figured out.

After the tribute, the girls disappeared, and the pageant began. Ursula and I did our usual banter and a number that we had barely rehearsed, but we were professionals and had the audience in the palm of our hand.

The girls came out for the swimwear competition, and they were all lovely. But as soon as she walked out on stage, Karen, with her long legs and willowy figure, was the surprise. She owned the runway, and when she left, the rest of the girls failed to compare.

"Well, Ursula? Why aren't you in your swimsuit tonight?"

"Honey..." She deepened her voice as far as it

would go. "Honey... I'm not getting paid nearly enough to show all that. What about you?"

"This is my swimsuit." I stood there in a black pantsuit with sequins on it. "Trust me, no one wants to see anything else. Even my boyfriend, Sheriff Hottie over there, asks me to keep my clothes on."

"Please, Ms. Skinny. I doubt that. Remember, I've been staying with you." She looked out at Harper, who bent his head and smirked. "Oh, he's blushing."

"No, girl. He's praying I keep the clothes on. Alright, Ladies and laddies who want to be ladies, it is my favorite time of the night. The evening gown competition and then we will take a short break as the judges tally their scores and we crown the new Ms. Cali West Coast. I, for one, will be so glad when this is over. I am tired."

"How do you think I feel? I haven't worked this hard since being kidnapped." The audience all laughed. They knew her story. It had aired all over our TVs even before her reality show.

The girls came on one by one, and Cory described their dresses with the cards they had provided him to read. I had always thought this was a weird part of pageant life. There were only so many ways to describe a dress. But he gave it his all.

I glanced up to the booth where he was standing and was surprised to find another figure there with him. Whoever it was, he was standing very close to him. Cory had been holding out on me, I think. I squinted cause I'm nosy, but all I could see was a manly shadow with wide shoulders.

The girls were all beautiful. Their gowns were exquisite, and their pageant hair was seriously on point. I mean, works of hair art, baby. Those wigs defied gravity, piled up on top of their head in curls and patterns that made me the hairstylist in me gag. Once again, Karen, Judy, Eatta, and Pam wore it best. The winner was hard to guess. All of the girls did well, but these four had risen to the top. Vivienne looked stunning, her cast bedazzled and sequined to match the gown, but this was not her year.

In the end, all the girls walked back out on stage and bowed. They held their fists up in solidarity, and Ursula and I looked at each other and choked back the tears. These were our sisters, and they were standing together.

We took a short break for the judges to discuss. I went down and sat beside Harper and Betty.

"You know Victor. This pageant has been statewide news. I was wondering if your man here was going to be able to solve the case." She smirked. "Once again, he and Vicki Dean were able to figure it out. I figured she would be here tonight."

"I guess she was too tired. You'd have to ask Harper or Cory. I rarely talk to her. She's nice enough, I guess. But I'm glad she was able to help. I've been a hot mess. Drag queens are not made for this kind of shit." I rolled my eyes, and she grinned at me.

"Oh, I think you've always been made of stern stuff, my friend. Oh, look. The new mayor is here tonight. You think he would have shown up if you hadn't solved the case? I should see if he'll give me a sound bite. Sneaky bastard."

She stood up and strode off, and I leaned my head on Harper's shoulder. "I love you," he said sweetly as he stroked my painted face.

"I don't want to get in drag for the next year." I sighed. "I'm so tired."

"You're beautiful, and I hope you know how thankful I am for you, baby."

We sat there holding each other's hand in silence for a while before I had to head back to the dressing room. When I entered, I found Cory and Jensen all cuddled up together talking to Ursula, and I almost spit my drink out all over the floor. Jensen? He was hot as crap, and Cory deserved a sweet man like him, but... God, did this mean we would have to double date? He was one of Harper's best friends.

He caught my eye and smiled.

"How long has this been... you know?"

"Since the pageant," Cory said coyly. "I thought I would wait to... you know, see where it went."

"Jensen... If you hurt him. I will murder you." I said seriously.

"Too soon..." Ursula laughed. "Honey, we have five minutes before we're supposed to be out there. You're changing, right?"

"I need to give the girls places. Coming?" He pulled Jensen behind him, who was grinning from ear to ear.

"I didn't even know he was gay." I shrugged.

"Honey, he looks like that. Of course, he is."

Ursula helped me change into my crowning gown, which was so beautiful I hated to even put it on. It deserved a special place in a museum instead of on me. I changed wigs really quick and glanced at myself.

We may be crowning a winner, but I felt like I won, too. Cory announced last year's winner, and she gave her swan song performance before a new Ms. Cali West Coast would be crowned. The audience apparently loved her and screamed for her as she finished.

We all walked out, and the girls held hands as they stood across the stage.

"The second runner-up is..." A drum roll came from the speakers. "Pam From Payroll."

All of the girls kissed her, and Cory handed her a bouquet of flowers.

"The first runner-up and the person who would have to fulfill the duties of the winner, if the winner is unable to is..." The drum roll sounded again. "Judy Ghouland."

Cory handed her a larger bouquet of flowers, and she went to stand next to Pam. I saw that they linked hands.

"The winner and your new Ms. Cali West Coast is..." The drum roll came out distorted, and everyone giggled. "Ooh, child... That was rough. The winner is Karen!"

All of the girls applauded and kissed her, throwing their arms around her in a big pile of hair and lee press-ons. I took a moment and blew a kiss to Ursula. We got through it and somehow survived this night-mare. The girls, for the first time in a pageant's history, seemed genuinely happy for the winner.

They were going to party hard tonight. They had survived. The crowd was on their feet as Karen bent down, and Ursula placed the crown upon her head and slid the sash over her dress. She looked ethereal, and tears of joy flooded down her face.

It was over.

Now I needed to finish my damn book.

THE END

<u>Drag Queen Detective #1</u>

Men Murder and Makeup (Drag Queen Detective #1)

Murder is a Drag.

Victor has a secret identity, and she's being framed for murder.

Murder She Wrote... If Jessica Fletcher were a Fabulous Drag Queen

The mayors been murdered and everyone is on edge and reclusive mystery author Vicki Dean is the prime suspect.

Can Victor clear her name without revealing his secret identity?

Will the hunky new sheriff help Victor prove Vicki's innocence or be a threat to not only his freedom but also his heart?

Victor must let go of his fear and step out of the

shadows in his high heels and lipstick to solve this mystery as only a drag queen can.

His life depends on it!

Drag Queen Detective #3

____

Himbos, Homicide and Heels

Hollywood is calling and they want Vicki Dean to play
the part of victim!

Powerful Hollywood agent and producer Marcus
Montrose has invited Vicki Dean and her friends to a
remote chateau in the Northern California mountains.
As soon as they arrive a blizzard cuts them off from the
rest of the world.

Trapped with some of Hollywood's greatest stars
sounds like fun, until the first body is found. It's a race
against the clock to discover which of the guests might
be a murderer.

With her boyfriend Harper Wolfe in tow, she takes it
on herself to solve the mystery. If she doesn't she or
one of her friends may be next. Can she get the

Himbos and starlets to reveal their secrets before it's too late?

The only thing she hates more than a dead body, is being stuck in drag for 48 hours!

236

Exes, Extortion and Eyeliner

Someone knows Vicki Dean's secret and they want her to pay – with her life!

When Victor got the first letter, it held a veiled threat. The second one demanded money. When the third arrived with a deadly threat to those he loves, he begins to uncover the truth.

Who's discovered that Victor is actually famous mystery novelist, Vicki dean? Can she discover their identity before they follow through with their threats?

How far will they go to destroy her?

Victor's not safe. With his ex-boyfriend showing up in town to supposedly make amends, his world is thrown upside down. Victor's hunky boyfriend, Sheriff Hottie and his best friend Cory do everything to protect him, but how can you protect anyone when you may be the next victim?

Drag Queen Detective #5

Sailors, Strangulation and Sunsceen

On the Rainbow Journey cruise to Alaska, everyone is having a blast – everyone, that is, except for the corpse. Trapped on a cruise ship with a killer isn't fun for anyone.
Victor and Harper have to find the murderer before they can strike again.
In the VIP suites a killer is on the loose. The Seeker of the Seas, an LGBTQIA+ cruise line is hosting a large group of partiers and the fun is starting to become deadly. Hoping to get a vacation - Victor, Harper, Cory and Jensen are excited to get out of Maple Bay and let loose. But someone else has other plans. Soon Victor and his friends are thrown into another mystery that they have to solve before anyone else gets hurt.

The VIP guests are keeping their secrets. Can Victor find out the truth or will he have to call on Vicki Dean to help solve the mystery? You already know that answer.

About Shane K Morton

Shane lives in Studio city with his husband and their fur babies, Bette Davis and Izzie Gillespie. His novels include: The Trouble With Off-Campus Housing, Private Waterloos, The Year of the Cock, Fault Lines, Bluegrass Boys Series and The Point Pleasant Holiday Series. His Dark Romance books, written under Sean Azinsalt, include: It's in My Blood, Bound, Dark Eros. When not writing, Shane can usually be found at a film festival or performing cabaret in a dark dive bar.

Join Shane's Facebook Group- Shane's Sweet and Salty Readers or join the mailing list to stay up to date on new releases at www.shanekmorton.com

9 798869 318664